Isn't he going to shut off? Jeff wondered. Ricky was beside him now and both riders were tucked low trying for speed. Their motors were screaming to the limit. Only fifty yards and they'd be there.

They passed the point where it was usual to brake and slow down for the first hill, but Ricky wasn't backing off.

This is crazy! Jeff was riding over his head and he knew it. In desperation he clamped on his brakes, hoping to end the dangerous game of chicken before it was too late.

But Ricky, like a Kamikaze pilot, did just the opposite, gearing up and gaining speed on a direct collision course with the Double Jump!

Mystery Rider at Thunder Ridge

DAVID GILLETT

Chariot Books
David C. Cook Publishing Co.

A White Horse Book
Published by Chariot Books,
an imprint of David C. Cook Publishing Co.
David C. Cook Publishing Co., Elgin, Illinois 60120
David C. Cook Publishing Co., Weston, Ontario

MYSTERY RIDER AT THUNDER RIDGE
© 1988 by David Gillett

Cover illustration by Paul Turnbaugh
Cover design by Loran Berg
First Print, 1988
Printed in the United States of America
92 91 90 89 88   1 2 3 4 5

Library of Congress Cataloging-in-Publication Data

Gillett, David.
  Mystery rider at Thunder Ridge.

  (A White horse book)
  Summary: Jealousy of a new motocross rider creates
problems for Jeff with his best friend and potential
girlfriend until he learns to deal with his attitude.
  [1. Motorcycle racing—Fiction] I. Title.
PZ7.G404My 1988   [Fic]   87-27846
ISBN 1-55513-398-3

Contents

1
Pre-season Dreams

It was 6:30 a.m. and Jeff Scott was nervous.

He stood at the foot of his driveway, anxiously toying with the strap on his red motocross helmet and looking up the deserted, early-morning street. The sun was climbing quickly into position above the dark green hills east of Jamestown. It made him groan mentally. *It's going to be a scorcher today. Just what we don't need!*

It was Saturday, and that meant race day for Jeff. Only this Saturday was a special one. He was sweating already. School would be out in less than a week, and the racing season would then begin in earnest. Today, during the 80A race, the race director would be picking three boys to go to the district racing camp at Thunder Ridge Motocross Park.

Going to the racing camp was an honor that Jeff had dreamed about for months. *Today is do or die,* he thought.

He ran long fingers through his wavy, jet black hair. He was tall and could have been a basketball player, or maybe a good left fielder, but ever since he'd been given his first BMX bicycle, he'd wanted to race motocross more than anything. His only problem, and he knew it, was nerves. His mother had always told him to pray about things and then forget them, but Jeff would only worry more. And he was worried now.

"Kaw-um-bah!"

Jeff nearly jumped out of his racing gear when the MacAttack's war cry broke the morning air just two feet behind him.

"Why don't you keep it down?" he said, turning to Randy MacLean ("MacAttack" as he was call by his friends). "The whole neighborhood's asleep!"

"*Was* asleep!" said Randy as he whipped his Redline BMX bike around and tried to pedal a wheelie across the paved driveway. He came down hard, narrowly missing Jeff's gleaming Honda.

As he watched his friend's antics, Jeff grinned. *Randy is weird. But is he ever a good rider. A good rider and a good friend.*

"Randy, you're weird!" said Jeff, careful not to add his thoughts about good rider and good friend. "Do you realize that in three hours we'll be on the starting line for maybe the most important race of the season?"

"The race to the Coke machine?" said Randy in a "little-kid's" voice.

"Yea, right! Oh, come on—this is the big race and you and I both have to do well, I mean like . . . win!"

"I'm afraid we can't both win, my son," said Randy in a fatherly voice. "You'll just have to be a man and accept third place."

"Third?"

"That's right, my lad, behind me and Suzanne, the girl that does sign-in!"

With that, Randy let another MacAttack war cry go and rode his bike into Jeff's garage where he stored his 80cc Suzuki.

A red van turned slowly onto Jeff's street. It had "Jamestown Honda" painted on the side.

"Here comes Art and his dad," said Jeff to Randy, "late as usual. The guy drives so slow it's ridiculous!"

"Like father, like son, I guess!"

There was truth to that. Art wasn't a very fast rider, but he tried hard. He had frizzy brown hair, shotgun freckles, and a fun-loving manner that made him an easy guy to be friends with. His dad, Mr. Brenner, always gave Jeff and Randy a lift to the races. He was already in their good book because he owned the local motorcycle shop.

As always on race day mornings, the job of loading Randy's and Jeff's bikes was a hassle. The van was big enough for their bikes and Art's, but Mr. Brenner always brought spare tires, extra gas, a pop cooler, lawn chairs with umbrellas—and his own motorcycle. He raced the old bike—a bigger 250cc—in the "Old-Timer's Class."

"Do you know who this van reminds me of?" said Randy, after the last piece of equipment was squeezed in and the back door jammed shut.

Art, smiling, took his cue and asked, "No, Randy, who *does* this van remind you of?"

"Charlene Johnson."

"Charlene Johnson?"

"Yeah. Do you remember last week when I stacked the books in her locker and everything came dumping out on top of her!"

I wish he'd get serious for once! Jeff was all business, and jokes from the MacAttack only made him realize just how on edge he really was. *Besides*, he thought, *Charlene Johnson is a nice girl*.

But he didn't think about her after that. He didn't have time. As he sat on the jiggling toolbox in the back of the van, wedged between Art's Honda, his own, and Randy's Suzuki, he planned his strategy for the day, deaf to Randy's constant talk with Art and Mr. Brenner.

He knew he could win the big 80A race if three things went his way: if Ricky Jackson had a bad day, if MacAttack got a poor start, and if his own bike ran well.

He'd raced at the Three Hills Raceway for two years already, ever since his dad had given in and agreed to let him join the Junior Racing program, so he knew the racetrack inside and out. He knew exactly how long it way—1 mile and 175 yards. He'd

10

memorized every turn, and he knew every jump—he knew just where to take off and where to land.

He looked over at Randy, and it was like he was watching TV with the sound off. Randy and Art were talking a mile a minute, but Jeff wasn't listening. He was thinking.

Randy wasn't anything special to look at, except maybe for his stringy blond hair that was always in his blue eyes. He was a lot shorter than Jeff who was tall for a fourteen year old. But the girls all liked Randy and even more so, it seemed, because Randy let on he didn't like them!

Randy was a real mystery to him alright. *A weird guy but a good friend,* he found himself thinking again. Then his mind forced him to admit, *and a real hot rider, too.*

He didn't know how Randy did it. Randy had a way of kidding around with everybody, telling jokes and cracking funny remarks, even as they'd line up at the start of a race, maybe thirty riders across. The "one-minute" board would be up and Randy would be using his "European" accent, making like some famous Swedish motocross star, telling his patented hamburger jokes and giving everybody fits of laughter.

Some riders called him "The Jitters Killer." He had a way of relaxing people and he didn't take racing too seriously.

But on the track, Randy was MacAttack all the way. Nobody in the 80A class at Three Hills could ride with him except Jeff—and Ricky Jackson.

11

Ricky Jackson. Jeff felt the butterflies building in his stomach just thinking of the name. The Yamaha rider who lived only three blocks from Jeff was loud-mouthed, always bragging, sometimes a cheater—but a very fast motocrosser.

Apparently his concern was showing.

"I know who Jeff's thinking about!" announced Randy with a sly smile. Jeff was jolted back into reality.

"Charlene Johnson?" said Art, teasing. Jeff's face reddened.

"Nope. Somebody even prettier than her," answered Randy. Jeff frowned.

"Brent Wade?" said Mr. Brenner, referring to the motocross pro who Jeff always cheered for and read about.

"Nope," said Randy, grinning wider. "Somebody even faster than Brent Wade, the superstar!"

"Who, then?"

"Ricky Jackson!"

At the name, Art screwed up his face and made a strange sound. His dad honked the horn.

"My kind of hero!" said Art laughing.

"Our kind of problem!" said Randy, slapping Jeff on the knee.

"Well, it's true, you know!" said Jeff, staring Randy in the eye. He was serious.

"Listen," he continued. "You know what could happen. Even if two of us place better than Ricky today, he might pull a third and we might have to bunk with him at racing camp. That sure would be

12

rotten. It would ruin everything!"

Randy was thinking. He realized that Ricky could be a problem, and he, too, was concerned.

Jeff looked at Randy and Randy looked straight back.

"And if he *wins*," said Randy, "that's all we'll hear about at racing camp for a whole week!" For once Randy wasn't joking.

Maybe he can get serious after all. Jeff's mind was working overtime. *If it worries Randy it must really be bad!*

"He cheats, you know," yelled Art from the front seat.

"Watch out," said Mr. Brenner. "You can't prove that."

"Well, I've seen it. I've seen him cut through that bumpy corner at the back of the track where there's no flagman."

"I knew it!" Jeff was angry. Then he smiled. "Look," he said to Randy in a low voice, "if we could cut that back corner, too, and beat him at his own game, maybe he wouldn't get sent to the camp."

Randy, the fun-loving, burger-eating MacAttack, was quiet. He fastened and unfastened the velcro closure on his red tennis shoe. Something was happening inside his wild blonde head.

He looked up at Jeff and smiled.

"I've got a better plan," he said at last. "I'll explain it when we get to the track."

The half-hour ride to the Three Hills Raceway

13

seemed like a lifetime to Jeff.

After leaving Jamestown, they swung past Riley Lake and drove around the abandoned quarry where most Jamestown riders practiced when they couldn't get to a real racetrack.

Then it was out to the highway and past a string of hamburger places. Each time they passed one, the MacAttack, like a radar beeper, would yell "Kaw-um-bah!"

Soon, Mr. Brenner's van twisted onto the roller-coaster road that led off the highway into hill country. They were part of a convoy now, a parade of pickups, vans, and cars with trailers, all of them on their Saturday morning trek into dirt-bike country.

Suddenly an airhorn blasted and Mr. Brenner swerved. A gleaming motor home, the size of a small ship, sailed past in a smoking rush.

"Tunesmith Racing," said Mr. Brenner, "never heard of *them* before."

"Number 68, Adam Bylow," said Art, reading the rider's name printed boldly on the motorhome's rear panel. "Never heard of *him* before, either."

"He ees likely zee World Champion of Motocross," said Randy in his worst French accent.

"Probably some hotshot from the city with a big bike," commented Jeff, hardly noticing. "He's sure to be riding in the 250-class." Right now he was more concerned about the butterflies doing warm-ups in his stomach. *One hour to racetime.*

That hour seemed like a minor lifetime. The sun was climbing in the sky and the water truck couldn't

14

spray fast enough to keep the dust down on the Three Hills Raceway. *Great*, thought Jeff, *with all this dust, Ricky will be sure to cheat and nobody will see him do it!*

Walking through the busy racing pit after their practice-session, Jeff, Randy, and Art passed the mystery motorhome that had rushed by earlier that morning.

"What a set-up!" said Art.

And it was. Air-conditioning, tinted windows, nice paint, the works.

Randy took a studied look: "Adam Bylow, eh? The guy must be a pro. Let's watch for him during the expert class races this afternoon. . . ."

Jeff wasn't interested. Mentally he was going through the motions of starting the race: let out the clutch gradually, drop it when the gate falls, roll on the throttle, shift up fast, don't get caught in first-turn traffic, stay ahead of the dust. . . .

A P.A. announcement broke his concentration: "Attention in the pits . . . 80A riders to the line . . . gate time five minutes. . . ."

"This is it, lads," said Randy, standing erect, holding his helmet over his heart and saluting the P.A. tower. "This is the moment of truth when all great burger-men stand to the test!"

"Shut-up!" said Art, smiling.

But Randy was rolling by now. "It's time to separate the men from the boys, and the boys from Jeff!"

"Knock it off!" said Jeff, fastening his helmet.

15

"This is where the going gets tough and the tough get sent to racing camp!"

Jeff was nervously cleaning his goggles. "Look— just be serious for a second and tell me what this great plan is for stopping Ricky Jackson."

"A Great Wall of Hamburgers in turn five."

"Be serious!"

"Are you sure you can handle it? It's a radical idea."

"Anything!"

"Well, here it is: let's both go out there and ride faster than him."

"Come on. . . ."

"Too radical for you? I thought it would be."

Jeff rolled his eyes and shrugged. "Too obvious is what it is."

"Well, it's also obvious that there's no other way to beat him. Do you think Brent Wade got to the top by putting out booby traps, sticking bubblegum in carburetors and getting Wiley Coyote to switch direction markers on the backstretch?"

Jeff shook his head. "You're class A squid!"

Randy just grinned.

The boys pushed their bikes to the starting gate. Art as usual, picked a spot on the outside, out of the thick of the action. *The also-ran position*, thought Jeff. Randy, the MacAttack, chose an odd spot: right beside Ricky Jackson.

Jeff was puzzled: *What's he going to do? Tell him a joke when the gate drops and hope he blows the start?*

16

Jeff rolled up to his favorite start position, right on the inside, the best place for winning the drag-race to turn one, also the most dangerous place to be if you weren't careful. But as he lowered his goggles and fired up his Honda, a rider with spanking new riding gear and a hot-looking bike, elbowed his way in beside him, taking over the inside spot.

A man beside this other rider, maybe his father, was yelling and pointing at a line down the racetrack.

If it hadn't been too late to do something, Jeff would have told the new rider not to butt in. But the ten-second board was up.

Just then, Jeff realized that the racer beside him was number 68. *Adam Bylow! In our race?*

2

Loser's Blues

That was as close to Adam Bylow as Jeff, or anybody, was going to get.

When the creaking gate dropped, sending thirty determined riders down the long dusty straight to the first turn, the flashy new rider pulled away like he'd been launched from a missile silo.

Jeff, trying to concentrate on first-turn traffic, was stunned. *What's going on here? This new guy might bump me off the list for camp!*

The race ran predictably: it began with two frenzied laps where everyone, even "also-rans" like Art, fought tooth-and-nail for position. The first two laps, raced handlebar to shoulder-pad, were usually the most dangerous, and Jeff worked hard to get out in front, ahead of the dust cloud generated by the snarling pack of jostling riders.

MacAttack and Ricky weren't in sight and Jeff didn't dare slow down to look behind him.

Blasting past the pit row on his third lap, he read the chalkboard signal that Mr. Brenner held out for him: "2, + 5."

That meant he was in second place with a five-second lead over third. But one thing was missing. Normally, when Jeff was riding in second, Mr. Brenner would scribble "Go for it." This time he didn't. Adam Bylow was too far gone for anyone to catch.

The race wore on. Only once did he catch sight of Adam Bylow; on a long straight stretch at the back of the track—but he was just a dusty bump in the distance, separating himself further from second place with every rut, jump, and turn.

At the midway point, Jeff's legs and arms were going rubbery, reminding him that this was just his fourth race of the season, and he wasn't yet conditioned for the gruelling pace. *Adam Bylow must have trained down south all winter!* he thought.

Mr. Brenner's pit board read "2, + 1" now. Jeff could hear a motor closing on him fast and he hoped it was the MacAttack. But he soon realized that it was Ricky Jackson's screaming Yamaha.

The two rivals headed down the long straightaway, past the announcer's tower and small grandstand from which parents and friends watched.

Jeff hated this part of the course. The reason loomed closer and closer: The Double Jump. Two small hills, separated by a valley about thirty feet across, were the main feature on this portion of the racetrack and few of the 80A class riders had tried to jump them. Some riders on more powerful motorcycles in other classes could do it, but for the 80A riders (even fast ones like Jeff and Ricky) the best thing to do was slow down and take them one at a time.

Fifty yards and they'd be there. Ricky was beside him now and both riders were tucked low trying for speed. Their motors were screaming to the limit.

Isn't he going to shut off? thought Jeff, wondering if Ricky was thinking the same thing.

They passed the point where it was usual to brake and slow down for the first hill, but Ricky wasn't backing off.

This is crazy! Jeff was riding over his head and he knew it. In desperation he clamped on his brakes, hoping to end the dangerous game of chicken before it was too late.

But Ricky, like a Kamikaze pilot, did just the opposite, gearing up and gaining speed on a direct collision course with the Double Jump!

Jeff's spirits sank as he watched his rival fly into the air off the first hill and land thirty feet away on the other side of the gulley—smoothly!

He couldn't believe it. *Ricky's on his way to racing camp for sure with riding like that!*

He rode through the Double Jump valley more slowly than usual.

Then, like act two from the script for a bad

20

dream, another rider on a bright yellow Suzuki, soared through the air on his left, clearing both hills in one shot, bumping Jeff back into fourth place. It was the MacAttack!

He was angry. *How could he do this to me? He made me look slow in front of everybody!*

Adrenalin surged through his arms and his right wrist twisted down hard on the Honda's throttle. He didn't want to lose another position.

But it didn't really matter now, he realized. The pit board read "4, + 10" and he felt robbed. Only three boys would be chosen.

After the race, Adam Bylow was the talk of the pits, but he'd disappeared into the big motor home so fast that none of the Three Hills regulars had a chance to meet him.

Jeff, for one, was not even interested in meeting him, nor was he interested in talking to Randy.

His friend tried to break the ice. He tossed Jeff a can of lemonade and said, "Good race man! You held second for over half the race and with this new guy out there, that's like first place among the regulars. I didn't think I'd catch you!"

Jeff was unimpressed.

"Look, Jeff—what's eating you? You rode great, and anyway, the Race Director won't pick just for finishing position. He'll look for consistency, talent, and smart riding."

"Was it smart to jump the doubles?" blurted Jeff, in a minor rage.

"It *was* kind of scary!" admitted Randy.

"And dumb! You made me look like a real slug out there—in front of everybody!"

Randy set his duffle bag down and turned to his friend to explain, but Art (who had finished a surprising eighth) walked into the conversation.

"Hey, you guys—I was too far back in the dust to see it, but somebody told me that Ricky Jackson cleared the Double Jump today! I didn't think he had the guts!"

Jeff kicked Mr. Brenner's cooler, turned on his heel and walked away with a red face.

Randy shook his head and rolled his eyes. "Right on cue," he said to a puzzled Art. "Perfect timing, Bozo!"

Later in the day, when Mr. Brenner limped in with seventh in an eight-rider Old-Timers' race, the Race Director held a meeting at the sign-in booth.

Sergeant Major, as the riders called him, was characteristically to the point.

"Good racing. Sorry about the dust, but our second pumper's in for repairs. As you know, Three Hills is sponsoring three of our top riders to the racing camp at Thunder Ridge. We're having a hard time deciding, but if we pick you, you'll get a call by next weekend. No races here next Saturday. Do some practicing."

Jeff, daydreaming, could see Ricky, Adam Bylow and Randy racing to their phones and grinning.

He and the others turned to leave, but stopped when Sergeant Major said, "And one more thing.

Thunder Ridge people tell me that besides their regular coach, Darrel Boyd, they've got Brent Wade coming for some special sessions at the camp. He's in the area anyway, getting ready for the big Super-cross race at Charger Stadium. He's a guy to watch!"

Brent Wade! Jeff felt the full weight of disappointment pushing in on him now. Not only was he going to miss racing camp, but his favorite pro rider would be teaching there.

Adding insult in injury, Ricky Jackson called across the parking lot: "Hey, Jeff, when you get on to riding a little bit better, try the Double Jump—it's a cinch!"

The next morning Jeff reluctantly rode to church with his parents. His dad, a policeman who worked odd shifts and had a hard time getting to Jeff's races, tried to pry under his son's hard shell of silence.

"So how did Art do yesterday at the race?"

"Okay, eighth."

"That's a good finish from him, isn't it?"

"I don't know. Yea, I guess so. He's usually about fifteenth. He was lucky."

"I'd sure like to get to one of your races sometime," said Jeff's dad, as they turned into the parking lot at Jamestown Community Church.

Yeah, sure you would, thought Jeff. *You'll do anything to arrange it so you can get to church, but you're always working on race day!*

"Yeah, dad, that would be nice," he said with an

icy voice, staring straight ahead.

Randy and Art both went to Jeff's church, although Randy had just started a few months ago. Jeff had never been excited about church, but it had been better lately with Randy coming. And Charlene. She was the best reason for going to church that he could think of.

"Hey, Jeff—get over the racetrack blues, yet?" called a familiar voice over the bustling crowd in the church lobby. It was MacAttack.

Jeff tried his best to ignore him, but he had to smile. *That guy is really weird! Where does he get his clothes?*

Jeff could never believe the way Randy dressed for church. Last week he'd worn a Boston Red Sox shirt. Today he had his "Team Suzuki" jersey on (the one with the hole in the right elbow).

He doesn't take church seriously, Jeff thought. *He thinks it's like racing, just a good time.*

The truth was, that for most of the boys in the junior high Sunday school class, church *was* a good time. Ben Masters, the teacher, was a great friend to everybody and on top of that he had a pool and an orange jeep that was great for trips to the beach.

And his Sunday school lessons were always interesting. He usually opened the class just talking with the boys about their week.

Jeff was quiet. He didn't share any news, especially about his black day at Three Hills Raceway.

Art, beaming, told about his eighth-place finish.

He's talking like he just won the Charger Stadium Supercross, thought Jeff, rolling his eyes.

Randy didn't mention how he'd finished the day before. But he did turn to Jeff and announce to the class in his best TV play-by-play voice: "And placing a strong fourth after almost pulling an upset over mystery rider Adam Bylow, is star rider Jeff Tension Scott. Tension, have you any thoughts about your fine performance?"

The MacAttack held an invisible microphone to Jeff's mouth, as the eight other boys in Ben Master's class waited for the Big Interview.

"No comment," he said with a forced smile. *If only they knew that a fourth was like a last yesterday,* he thought. But he had to laugh as Randy carried on with the interview giving Jeff's supposed answer in a terrible Swedish accent.

Just like at the races, a real space-cadet! But at least Jeff was smiling.

During the morning service, he forgot all about motocross. He was on pins and needles, lovestruck. He didn't hear the sermon and only mouthed the words to the hymns . . . the wrong words.

Charlene Johnson, who had always come to church, but had never spoken much to Jeff, had walked right over to him just a minute before the service and said, "Jeff, I just wanted to say I saw your race yesterday—it was great. Can you stay around for a minute after service? I want to ask you something."

Jeff had never really expected to see an angel up

close, but he'd just heard one speak. His mind was racing and his heart beat like a Honda in top gear.

He looked thoughtful during the sermon.

The fact was, his mind was overheating, trying to analyze Charlene's short speech. To think that she'd been at the racetrack and he hadn't known!

"I saw your race," she'd said. Did that mean she'd seen his racing, or the race as a whole?

"I thought it was great." Did she mean she'd thought *he* was great or Adam or Ricky or Mac-Attack?

"Can you stay around a minute after service?" He could stay around all day for her! All week!

And, finally, he mulled the last phrase over and over again: "I want to ask you something . . ." But what? What could Charlene, who had never seemed too interested in motocross or in Jeff, want to ask *him*? The tension was unbearable. Randy had been right. "Tension" was a good nickname.

Finally, when the longest sermon in Jeff's memory ended, he and Charlene met in the sunny parking lot.

This is it, he thought, as she spotted him and came over, looking a lot prettier than he'd ever remembered.

"Thanks for waiting around," she began. "That was only the second motocross race I've ever been to. I didn't realize you guys had to be such great athletes!"

Jeff tried to put an important sentence together, but gave up with a dry throat.

She continued. "I guess you know that this Friday night is the Youth Group's end-of-school wiener roast and pool party. We're having it at Ben Master's house over at Riley Lake. I really hope you can make it. Sherry, Linda and I are in charge of inviting people. Maybe you could help us phone everybody?"

"All right! I mean, yea! I'll help, of course," said Jeff in a daze. *Why should she ask me? But she did!*

Charlene, with fingers that betrayed a hidden nervousness, handed him a Youth Group list with a section of names and numbers circled in red. "Phone these kids," she said with a smile, "and then let me know how it goes."

And as she turned to leave, she stopped, and with a far-away look, said: "And maybe you could try to get that new racer to come. You know—Adam Bylow."

As she walked off, Jeff shoved the crumpled list deep into his pocket. "Oh, yeah, I know all right!" he said quietly.

3
Mystery Rider

An echoing knock sounded on Jeff's bedroom door. A far-away voice said "School, Jeff. Last Monday before holidays!"

But the early morning message slid quietly across his rumpled blankets, out his open bedroom window and disappeared.

Jeff's mind was in sleepy turmoil. A half-opened eye focused lazily on a full-color poster of Brent Wade, high in the air over a jump in the Los Angeles Coliseum. The other eye, closed and dreaming, watched Charlene walking away, her yellow dress flowing in the breeze. He watched the way her soft, brown hair bounced with every step. Then the rider on the poster faded into a likeness of Adam Bylow, and Charlene was running, and. . . .

"Jeff—your last Monday before summer vacation!" His mother repeated the message as she knocked again. "I've got breakfast ready."

And the last before racing camp. Why did I have to wake up dreaming about Adam Bylow?

"That Charlene is a nice girl. I know her mom," said Mrs. Scott at breakfast.

"I guess so," mumbled Jeff through his Wheaties.

"Well, I saw you talking to her at church yesterday."

"Yes," he replied abruptly. He was not talkative most mornings, and as he remembered Charlene's last request, he was silent.

He stayed that way as he rode his BMX bike to school. Art, on his 12-speed mountain bike, tore past with a challenge to race. Jeff shook his head and pedalled slowly. *Racing stinks*, he thought. *What does Art really know about racing?*

He drifted through his morning classes, and it was the same thing in each: review, review, review for a week of tests, tests, tests. But Jeff's mind was elsewhere—on race, win, lose. The more he thought about it, the worse he felt.

"My lads, eat hearty," said MacAttack at lunch, "for this Friday we party!"

The pool party at Ben's! "I don't know if I can make it," Jeff said, staring at MacAttack's tuna and marmalade sandwich.

"It's your diet," said MacAttack, handing half of the strange sandwich across the table, "Munch this wonder-lunch and you'll never need to worry again

29

about ill health or acne!"

"That's for sure," said Art. "You'll be dead!"

Jeff looked at the sandwich. He looked at Randy, the crazy MacAttack. He forgot about motocross and his face brightened.

"One small bite for mankind," he said, closing his eyes and biting in.

Jeff downed the tuna and marmalade concoction in front of the six boys. He licked his lips and said, "Could had used more soya sauce, but I'll give it an 8.5." And with that, the whole day changed. *A little craziness*, he thought, *sure makes you feel better*.

The conversation turned away from weird food to more weighty matters.

Art set the ball rolling: "Who can answer the big question? Who is this Adam Bylow guy?"

"Well," began MacAttack, deep in thought, "he's not a bird and he's not a plane, so he must be Super Bylow, the mild-mannered motocross racer who jumps large doubles in a single bound."

"Well, whoever he is, he probably stole my spot at racing camp," said Jeff.

MacAttack tried to sympathize, "Well, *maybe* he did, but you've got to admit it—the guy is F-A-S-T fast!"

Art added, "And talk about a nice set-up for going to the races. That motor home must be worth fifty grand at least! His dad must be loaded!"

At least his dad goes to the races with him, thought Jeff.

"I was talking to Ricky this morning in Math,"

said Art, changing the subject, "and he told me he heard that Town Council might lock the Quarry Pit to keep guys from riding there."

"That would be a drag," said Jeff.

"Bad news," said MacAttack.

"A disaster," said Art. "I mean, where could we take our motocross bikes to practice? It's not like we have a track close by, and besides, none of us will be able to drive for at least a year, so we couldn't get to the country anyway. Ricky says it's because there is somebody riding in there in the evening and on Sunday mornings when it's off-limits. He says we should try to find out who it is before it's too late."

"Any ideas?"

No one seemed to know who the mystery rider might be. Then Jeff slammed his fist on the table and exclaimed, "I bet it's that Adam Bylow jerk!"

"Why would he want to ride there," said Art, "when his dad could take him anywhere in that motor home?"

"Sure, but it would be just like him to try and get *our* riding area shut down so we have nowhere to practice!"

MacAttack looked at Jeff and frowned. "I say we can't jump to conclusions about the guy. And anyway, he doesn't need to do anything sneaky to get an edge on us. He's already about the fastest 80A rider I've ever seen!"

There was general agreement about that. But why was he so fast? Was it his bike? Did he work out at a health club? Did he ride in Florida all winter?

Was everybody else just *slow*?

On the way to his afternoon classes, Jeff was tapped on the shoulder in the crowded corridor. It was Charlene. He didn't have time to get nervous.

"Hi, Charlene."

"Hi, Jeff! How's the phoning going? Many kids coming to the party Friday night?"

Phoning! Jeff felt his palms go cold and clammy.

"Well," he stammered, stalling for time, "I haven't really called anybody yet—I mean it was just yesterday morning when you asked me."

"But don't forget that the party is just this Friday." She reached out and squeezed his arm as she said it. Then she turned and walked off, her light brown hair bouncing as it had in his early morning dream.

He could feel the warm finger prints on his arm, and as he was considering whether or not to ever wash his arm again, Ricky Jackson walked up beside him: "Nice babe—*very* nice; I hear she likes Superman Bylow. I guess we can't *all* be winners, Jeffrey!" Once more adding insult to injury, he reached out and gave Jeff's arm a vise-like squeeze exactly where Charlene had done so only seconds before.

Jeff, in that instant made up his mind about two things: Firstly, who he would and would not ask to the party and, secondly, whether he would wash his arm. The answer to the second question was yes—and with strong soap.

Friday, the last day of school, took forever to arrive. But when it came, the celebration followed hard on its heels. Next year it would be high school for Jeff and most of his friends, and that was at once exciting and scary.

Jeff's dad, who was supposed to drive him to Ben Master's place, was called down to the police station at the last minute.

"Sorry, Jeff," he said as he hurriedly collected his uniform and rushed to the door. "Your mother will have to give you a lift!"

"What else is new?" Jeff said as the door slammed and he heard his dad's thick police shoes running down the walk.

Later, as his mother drove him to the party, she said, "Look Jeff, your dad hates to break a promise to you."

"Sure!"

"Well, he does! And anyway, how would you like to have a father like your friend Randy? He hardly spends any time with his son at all—he just sits in front of the TV and drinks. Would you like a dad like that?"

Jeff didn't say another word. He watched Jamestown pass the windows of the car, watched as they swung down by Riley Lake, past the old Quarry Pit and up the little hill to Ben Master's house.

"Call me when it's over," said Jeff's mom, giving him a squeeze on the arm as he opened his door to get out. He'd never realized before how many ways one arm could be squeezed!

Not many kids had arrived yet, and Jeff was early, as he was for most things—races, school, church—and, until recently, the checkered flag at moto-cross races.

Ben's house wasn't a big one—in fact, it was tiny—sort of like a one bedroom apartment with a shingled roof on it. But Ben lived alone and didn't need a lot of space, so it was plenty big for him. He'd put his extra money into building a nice pool, a sauna hut, and a garage for his orange Jeep.

Jeff liked Ben's place, and so did the rest of the kids from Jamestown Community Church. It was like a second home to a lot of them. They were always going over to swim and watch videos and play basketball on the pavement in front of the garage.

Charlene's best friend, Sherry, saw Jeff arrive and ran over.

If she squeezes my arm, I'll yell! he was thinking, smiling to himself.

"Just what we need," she began, "some muscles to help move the picnic table."

"Where's Ben?" asked Jeff.

"He's out with the jeep getting Randy and some of the guys. Charlene wanted me to ask you something," and she smiled that mischievous way girls smile when they ask a question on a friend's behalf. "She wants to know if you got Adam Bylow to come tonight!" Then with a giggle (a *stupid* giggle, thought Jeff) she squeezed his arm.

"Ahh!" he yelled, "That hurt!" And smiling a this-is-a-joke smile, he lied, "I called him . . . but he said

34

he was going on a date tonight."

"Oh, really?" she replied, and her voice showed that her friend would be disappointed.

The party at Ben's was a good one—a great one, in fact.

"Can you think of a better way to celebrate the last day of school?" Sherry asked the group after she'd handed Ben a giant thank you card signed by everyone.

"I can," said MacAttack.

Art nudged Jeff and whispered, "Watch this!"

Ben, with a suspicious smile, said "How?"

And MacAttack, setting down his Coke can on the poolside pavement let out his famous war cry and yelled, "With a Pool War!" and he lunged at Ben, grabbing Sherry by the wrist and taking both of them into the water in a startling flurry of flailing arms and legs.

Art, obviously in league with MacAttack, body-checked Jeff sideways into the water and soon everyone was in on the act, and into the pool.

It was good times like these and the spontaneous fun that Ben encouraged that helped make the youth group "click."

And there was a more vital ingredient that tied in nicely with every gathering. It was a natural extension of Ben's character—not a put on, just a part of his life that he shared with the kids who were his friends. He had a way of relating to the latest news—to the things that were happening in their lives. After the pool war and the wiener roast, he sat

35

down on the grass and talked with the group.

"Art was telling me about the problems over at the old Quarry Pit and how some of you guys are going to be out of luck because of one person's inconsideration. I think it all boils down to a lack of respect for authority!"

"It's one thing to joke around and have a good time" (he threw some dandelion stems at Randy as he said it) "but when it comes to disobeying laws, it's rebellion against not only man, but God, too. I've heard a bike over there at night before and I know why Town Council is concerned. Not only is that person making noise after hours, but he could get hurt and be in danger personally."

Ben went on to point out how Jonah almost caused disaster because he rejected God's authority. "As a result of his disobedience," Ben said, "Jonah jeapordized the lives of a whole ship's crew, and he ended up nearly dying in the belly of a whale."

Randy spoke up, "So are you saying that if we find this guy—whoever he is—riding at the Quarry Pit, we should throw him overboard—into the pool?"

Jeff, sitting beside Charlene, laughed along with everyone else, but he was feeling a bit guilty for having lied about Adam. He almost wondered if he should tell her the truth.

She'd probably never talk to me again, he thought, and kept quiet.

Later, he was helping Ben and the girls clean up, when the phone rang. It was Jeff's dad.

"He's probably calling to say he can't come to get me," he said as he took the receiver from Ben.

"Jeff," said his dad from the other end of the line, "just after I got in tonight, I got a really special phone call."

"What was it?" asked Jeff impatiently.

"Do you remember when you were little how I used to buy you a 'passing-present' each year when school ended if you did okay on your grades?"

"Yeah. What are you getting at?"

"Well, this is this year's passing-present —Sergeant Major, as you boys call him, called from Three Hills to say you're going to racing camp; you, Randy and Ricky."

Jeff was silenced.

"Jeff!" said his dad's voice, distant and scratchy, "Jeff?"

"Yes, dad. But what about Adam Bylow?"

"Who's he?" said Jeff's dad, meaning it.

In a daze, Jeff slammed down the receiver and ran outside, ready to take on the world. He had his T-shirt half off when he reached the pool and said to Ben, "I want to take a swim to celebrate!" but before Jeff could explain himself or jump in, Ben stopped him and said, "Be quiet—listen!"

And through the darkness, from the direction of the old Quarry Pit, came the high lonely whine of a well-tuned 80cc motocross bike running through the gears.

4

Thunder Ridge Camp

"This is *pretty strange*, Tension!" said the MacAttack.

"Definitely different," echoed Ricky Jackson.

"But F-A-S-T fast!" said Jeff as he climbed into the van parked in his driveway.

It was not Mr. Brenner's "Jamestown Honda" van or the van that Rick's dad sometimes drove. It was a blue and white van with "Jamestown Police Tactical Unit" painted boldly on the side.

Sunday had arrived, and the three riders were on their way to racing camp at Thunder Ridge with Mr. Scott as their chauffeur.

"When Jeff found out he was going to camp," began Mr. Scott, "he dropped the receiver and nearly broke my eardrum! But I decided I'd give you guys a ride anyway, since it's my day off. And why not go in style?"

"So, we take the SWAT van!" laughed Ricky, "*Style* is right!"

Jeff and MacAttack sat side by side in the van, facing Ricky, their motocross bikes between them. Neither one said much. How could they talk freely with their racetrack rival sitting across from them?

Jeff's dad called back: "Hey, Jeff—I was wondering—who's this Adam Bylow you mentioned when I called?"

That broke the ice and started all three riders talking.

"A jerk who gets anything he wants," said Ricky.

"But a jerk who can beat anybody at Three Hills," said MacAttack.

"Why wasn't he chosen for the camp, then?"

Jeff piped up without hesitation: "Because he's a show-off."

Insightful Randy, the MacAttack, put things straight and they all knew it, "Really it's because he's not a Three Hills regular. Sergeant Major said he wanted riders to represent *his* track, and that's what we, my dear gentlemen, are about to do."

The trip was a long one, punctuated by brief stops at burger shops and gas stations. Their route took them at one point along the eight-lane freeway that by-passed the big city.

"See that white dome on the horizon, to the left of those two radio towers?" said Jeff's dad, "That's the top of Charger Stadium. It's an air-suspended roof,

39

a completely enclosed football stadium."

"Football nothing!" exclaimed Ricky. "That's where the Supercross is being held a week from Friday night. I'd give anything to go to that!"

Jeff and MacAttack felt likewise. Although they both read all of the monthly racing magazines and watched motocross on TV, they'd never been to a stadium race before.

Jeff's mind flipped back to the half-waking dream he'd had almost a week earlier. Once again he could see Brent Wade flying high off a supercross jump in the Coliseum. But he stopped the mental videotape when he reached the part where Brent faded into Adam Bylow.

I'll never get dad to take me to that race, he thought. *He's almost always on duty on Friday night.*

Then Ricky, like a mind-reading machine on a time-delay, called to Mr. Scott: "Hey, Mr. Driver, do you think you could take us to the Supercross race a week from Friday?"

Jeff rolled his eyes, looked at Ricky, and shook his head as if to say, "Not a chance."

His dad answered, "Only if you guys take an apple to your teacher, do your homework, and sit up straight in class. Seriously, though, I'll see if I can change my shift. That might be a holiday weekend anyway."

"Not a chance," Jeff whispered to MacAttack, "not a chance!"

Just the same, the boys toyed with the exciting

possibility of going to the Supercross race. And with only half an hour left before reaching Thunder Ridge, Jeff and Randy began to realize something that had never seemed even remotely possible: Ricky wasn't such a bad guy after all.

In fact, he was a pretty good guy. Ricky told them how he practiced hard all week and ran two miles every morning before doing his paper route.

"You mean you run and *then* you do a paper route?" asked MacAttack. "How many burgers do you have to eat to get that much energy?"

And Ricky told them how much fun he thought the three of them would have at the racing camp. He sounded genuinely excited.

Jeff "Tension" Scott was feeling tense, and not just a little guilty. *"Judge not, that you be not judged,"* he thought, recalling one of Ben Master's talks about not pre-judging people, especially people you didn't know very well. But his tension changed focus completely as the Jamestown SWAT van turned through the gates of Thunder Ridge Motocross Park.

Thunder Ridge was a pretty impressive place— head and shoulders above Three Hills Raceway. There was a motel and restaurant, a complete motorcycle shop, a dining hall, and a three story announcer's tower. Only a glimpse of the actual racetrack could be seen from the entrance, but it looked promising: black, rich earth, well-groomed, between parallel rows of trackside banners.

"Gentlemen," began the MacAttack, winding up, "feast your eyes on *that* baby!" And he pointed across the lawn beside the dining hall to a large swimming pool surrounded by a red-tiled deck.

"Hit the beach!" yelled Ricky.

"Pool War Two!" yelled the MacAttack, tumbling out of the van even before Jeff's dad had brought it to a complete stop.

"Looks like a pretty good place, Jeff," said Mr. Scott as they watched MacAttack and Ricky run off to case the joint.

"Yeah, dad. Thanks for driving us!"

"No problem."

Jeff stood beside his dad, not saying much, but half-believing that maybe his dad *was* interested in his sport after all. As he pondered that thought, he nearly had to pinch himself to believe that he had actually arrived at racing camp after all the frustrating events of the previous week.

Two fellows in a mini-pick-up pulled up. "Nice paint job on the van," they hooted.

"It's for real," Jeff returned.

"Wow! Excellent!"

Jeff smiled at his dad and swelled with a pride he hadn't felt for a long time. But something inside gripped him, and held his tongue from saying anything more. He swung open the van's rear door and said, "I guess we should unload."

Mr. Scott put the ramps in place. "I'll unload your bikes and gear while you find out where you bunk and park your machines. When you're sorted out, come by and see me off."

Jeff caught up with his poolside friends. They were talking a mile a minute.

"We can use the pool anytime, except during classes."

"If we shower first."

"They've got a video arcade in the dining hall!"

"And Monster Burgers in the restaurant!"

"That's great, guys," said Jeff, ever level-headed, "but what about the motocross school? Like, where do we register and sleep and all that?"

"Good point, Tension," said MacAttack. "We hadn't really given that any thought."

Other trucks, vans and motor homes were now arriving, with more uninitiated pupils. Seemingly out of nowhere, a P.A. voice scratched to life, "Racing camp registration will begin in fifteen minutes at the snack bar below the announcer's tower. Welcome to Thunder Ridge Motocross Park."

Jeff scanned the busy, gravelled parking lot, through a light cloud of powdery dust. He was looking for one thing—the bright blue and red box van with "Brent Wade" painted on the side.

The boys saw other riders whom they recognized.

"He's the guy that went through the snowfence on turn 5 last month," snickered Ricky, pointing at a boy with red hair and checkered sunglasses.

Jeff recognized someone else, and felt the hair stand up on the back of his neck. He was dumbfounded. "What in the world is *he* doing here?" and he pointed to the gleaming Tunesmith Racing motor

43

home, as it pulled through the gates.

"*He* didn't get picked," said a puzzled MacAttack.

Ricky offered a solution that made Jeff even more edgy, "Maybe Adam Bylow is in love with the promoter's daughter or something!"

Or something, thought Jeff and the mental video was rolling again—Adam Bylow high in the air in the Coliseum, Charlene running after him and away from Jeff. Jeff felt as though he hated Adam. But then he reprimanded himself—*This is crazy! I haven't even talked to him yet and he probably doesn't even know Charlene exists.*

"Am I ever stupid," he said out loud.

"What, Jeff?"

"I said let's meet the Superman, our hero!"

"We can play mind games with him," said Ricky, "just like the pros do, trying to psych each other out before the big race."

Adam Bylow turned out to be short and muscular, blonde and tanned, with the look of a surfer-turned-wrestler. *A girl killer*, thought Jeff, *a real Romeo.*

MacAttack introduced himself, and, in his usual way, was soon talking with Adam as though he was an old friend. Ricky and Jeff stood in the background, mouths open as Adams dad unloaded new riding gear and *two* motocross bikes.

"You completely smoked us at Three Hills," said MacAttack, having finally steered around to the topic of the week—racing.

"Well, I guess it was close," said Adam, oddly

44

nervous, glancing behind him at his father.

"Close? Are you kidding? You were also the first guy in our class ever to clear those doubles at the front of the track! You're great!"

Knock it off, Randy, Jeff was thinking.

Adam abruptly changed the subject. "Is there a pool here?"

"A big one, with a slide!"

"How about trails, for *hiking* on? I'm looking for wildlife photos."

Wildlife photos? Jeff was wondering how strange the Bylow case could get.

A loud voice sounded from the shady side of the motor home. It was a forceful, authoritative voice. "Adam, get your stuff in order. Business first, then you can talk to the others."

There was something odd about Adam's response —the way he turned from the MacAttack without a word. He disappeared into the motor home and slammed the door behind him. A cool gust of air rushed out.

"Air-conditioning and everything! The guy's got it made!" said Ricky, shaking his head.

MacAttack looked at Jeff. His eyes reflected the same puzzlement.

After a hectic registration and room assignment, the riders gathered in the dining hall for an introductory meeting, led by Darrel Boyd, the Camp Director.

Jeff knew who Darrel was and felt glad he was in charge of things. He was tall and lean, sort of a clean-cut cowboy, and he had been state motocross champion when Jeff had first become interested in the sport. Darrel had never made it big nationally. He wasn't a real *star* like Brent Wade. But he'd raced in Europe and worked as a test rider for a Swedish racing company. He was good, really fast and smart. Ben Masters had even told Jeff that he thought Darrel was a Christian.

We'll see about that, thought Jeff. But his mind wandered. Instead of listening to Darrel talk camp rules, he scanned the crowd for Brent Wade, wondering how he'd get an autograph on his racing jersey.

5

Mind Games

That evening, at the barbecue, MacAttack was in his element. The ingredients were all there: lots of people, a big pool and lots of hamburgers.

"How do they rate Mac?" asked Ricky, dissecting a burger and pulling the stringy onion slices out.

MacAttack took an educated bite and furrowed his brow in thought, then replied, "Not bad for amateurs—I'd give it an 8.9 on the burger scale."

"And they get worse, guys," said Darrel Boyd, joining the small group. "We call them Thunder-burgers around here!"

He introduced himself to the three Jamestown racers and was soon talking to them like an old racing buddy.

"I met your dad, Jeff," he said. "Couldn't miss

him. It's not every day a SWAT van pulls in here! He says that you boys all go to church together, is that right?"

Jeff looked at MacAttack but not Ricky.

"Well, Randy and I do," he said.

"That's great. Maybe you'd be interested in a special session I'm starting this year, sort of a pilot project. I'm calling it my 'Mind Power Option.' Every morning at 5:45 a.m., just before breakfast, I'm meeting on the racetrack starting line with anybody interested. Fifteen minutes of mind preparation before the start of the day. Interested?"

Ricky spoke up: "I guess so! Mind games are a big part of my strategy!"

Darrel looked at Jeff and MacAttack, "You two?"

"We'll be there," said MacAttack, "at least we will if the thunderburgers don't put us six feet under!"

Later, Darrel climbed onto a picnic table and called for attention.

"We're running a little late, but I wanted to give Brent some more time. We've got to get started so we'll go ahead without him. It seems he had to go into town for the evening."

A moan of general disappointment went up and Darrel continued.

"Anyway, Brent is going to teach the afternoon riding session tomorrow, so you're in for some *real* riding!"

He opened his clipboard and began to read from his notes. "Breakfast is at 6:15. At 7:30 we do bike prep for half an hour. Then we get to work." He hesitated, then added with emphasis, "And I mean *work!*"

Jeff could picture it now—he and Brent Wade riding wheel to wheel around the winding, groomed track, getting faster and faster with each lap. . .

"You've all got your roommates, and you guys who are camping should be set up by now. It's only 9:00 and I'm sure you're all ready for another swim, but let me tell you something. If you *do* stay up late tonight, you'll be *dead* after tomorrow's session, and I bet there won't be one of you awake at 9:00 *tomorrow* night!"

Sure enough, it was a late one. MacAttack, in league with two pranksters from the Baysville Motorsports Club, organized a riotous "Pool War" and started things off by throwing Darrel Boyd in—hamburger and all.

It was 11:30 before Jeff switched the light off in the tiny room he shared with Ricky Jackson.

In the dark he lay awake thinking. He thought about Charlene and about Adam Bylow and wondered how he'd ever survive a week with Ricky as his roommate. *This is like the plot from a bad movie,* he thought, trying to imagine who on earth could be a worse roommate than Ricky. Then he remembered the van ride earlier that day. *Maybe it will work out,* he thought.

"Where's the MacAttack sacking out?" said Ricky from the darkness of the lower bunk.

"I think he said he's with Dave and Jim Thomas.

They're those Kawasaki crazies from Baysville."

"It's a wonder he's not living in the motor home with Superman," Ricky said and added, "I think Mac must be taking some pointers from him. They spent a long time talking tonight."

Jeff could feel his fist tightening. He was conscious of the tension, but didn't know where it came from. He didn't feel at all like sleeping. *This is crazy: I'm supposed to be enjoying myself!*

Ricky kept talking. "Are you going to the Mind Power Option in the morning? 5:45 comes pretty early, but I'd eat five more thunderburgers if it would give me an edge over Superman Bylow!"

"I don't know . . ." Jeff answered. He wouldn't mind an edge also, but 5:45 was pretty early. . . .

At 5:44, Ricky was pulling at Jeff's sleeping bag? "Move it! One minute to gate time!"

They found Darrel sitting alone on the steel starting gate, and he was glad to see them. The morning was cool and the sun was only beginning to cut through the heavy mist that hung like a shroud over Thunder Ridge.

There was something unreal about it all, and Jeff felt like a pilgrim reaching the top of a mysterious mountain. If Darrel was the guru he'd come to see, he was a strange one. He wore a red track suit and soccer shoes with orange plastic-cleated soles. He hadn't combed his black hair, or at least it didn't look like it, and he, too, was feeling the effects of the late night before.

"I can't believe somebody actually made it!" he said.

"Me neither!" said Ricky, yawning.

Darrel looked around, shrugged, and began by saying, "It looks like just the three of us today." Then, without any warning or explanation, he said, "Let's pray."

Jeff and Ricky stared at each other, then Jeff looked away quickly and bowed his head. He didn't even hear what Darrel said—his face was burning with embarrassment. *What is this?* he was thinking, *Ricky will think we're crazy!*

Darrel said "Amen" and looked up, a sly smile on his face, a silent look that seemed to ask, "What do you think of that?"

Neither Ricky nor Jeff spoke, but fidgeted nervously and wished they were elsewhere. *This is weird*, thought Jeff, *this is really strange*.

Darrel broke into a grin. "You guys must be wondering about me right? *Praying* before a day of motocross?" He stood up and dragged his cleated shoe through the black loamy soil, making a line. "It's like this," he continued. "I'm on this side of the line, and you're on the other. I'm a pro rider, and a former champion. I make my living running motocross camps and racing part time. You guys are still in school and you've got a long way to go, but you want to be on my side of the line. You want my expertise and you're ready to work for it, but I don't think you're ready to go all the way to get it." Then he looked around again, at the deserted starting line and the silent buildings that were beginning now to pick up the long, sharp rays of early sunlight. "But it looks like you're more willing to try than the rest of these guys. I dare you both to be here tomorrow morning."

Jeff cringed. He was sure Ricky was going to make some rude comment and steam away. But instead, he slapped Jeff on the shoulder, stepped over the line and said, "Let's go for it!"

The three of them set off for the dining hall. Jeff started to jog. Ricky picked up the pace, and Darrel led them in an all-out run. Racing camp had started.

The morning moved quickly. Darrel and his two assistant coaches ran through a maintenance drill and the fifty-two motocross bikes were left cleaned, oiled and ready to go.

"Everybody walk their bikes to the starting gate and park them there, then go and get dressed for the first session. But not," and he spoke up as the riders turned to leave, "in riding gear. Put on your sweats and get back here on the double!"

The first session was a race all right. Darrel, in his red track suit, lined up amongst the boys behind the steel starting gate and counted down from ten, his hand on the gate lever. "When I get to 1, the motocross race of the century is on. One lap of the track—running all the way—no short cuts!"

The MacAttack, leaning over the gate and stretching his short legs, looked Jeff up and down. "This isn't fair," he said, looking at Jeff's long legs.

"It's like you've got two more gears than me!"

Darrel counted "3—2—1!" dropped the gate, and broke into a fast run down the long straight to turn one.

Jeff could see that he had some real running to do—he was already falling back as some sprinters tore past in pursuit of Darrel.

"C'mon, you Honda riders!" called Darrel, as he disappeared over *Riot Ridge* into *Mud Gulley*.

Through the mud-hole? thought Jeff.

"Through the mud-hole!" yelled MacAttack as he blazed by, unconcerned about clean shoes.

The Thunder Ridge track was exactly one mile long and it was the hardest mile Jeff has ever ran—mudholes, killer hills, sandy sections where everyone bogged down and tripped up.

When he finally took the last turn and ran wearily toward the announcer's tower, his heart sank even further. Sitting trackside sipping Gatorade was Darrel, Adam, and Ricky, long since finished with their lap. It looked like Ricky's training schedule had paid off for him. As for Adam, well. . . .

The fact that Jeff had beat MacAttack and more than two-thirds of the rest of the class was little consolation. *I'm glad Charlene wasn't at this race!* he thought, as Darrel stood up and jumped high in the air, waving a checkered flag.

"The winner!" Darrel announced.

"Not likely," said Jeff.

"No, really you are," replied Darrel, slapping him on the back. "Anybody who even finishes is a big

53

winner!" Darrel held out the limp black and white checkered flag to Jeff. "And you know what the winner gets to do with the checkered flag, don't you?"

"Yeah," yelled Ricky, "he gets to do a victory lap with it!"

Jeff didn't do a victory lap, but he did laugh, and he did join in the fun, giving a standing ovation to each runner as they finished. He was beginning to enjoy himself again.

Lunchtime came and went, a time of real hunger, real food and typical MacAttack hi-jinx. But the dining hall air was full of anticipation. Brent Wade would be conducting the first riding session of the week.

"After lunch," said Darrel, standing on a bench in the dining hall, "I want everybody in riding gear. We're going to have our first on-track session and right now I'd like to introduce our guest instructor, Brent Wade, who rides professionally and has . . . well, I guess you guys know everything about this man! Brent, it's all yours!"

Jeff could feel goose bumps rising on his arm and told himself, *he's just another rider*, but he knew that he'd always wanted to be like Brent Wade more than anybody else.

Brent stood on the bench where Darrel was.

Jeff recognized the face all right. How many photos of that face had he clipped from motocross magazines? It was Brent's height that surprised him. He'd always pictured Brent as at least six feet tall, but there he was in the flesh, and he was just about the same size as MacAttack, or . . . Adam.

Brent spoke with a slow, southern accent—not quite a drawl, but sort of. "So you guys want to be good, huh? Well this week I'm going to show you the only thing that stands between you and the checkered flag." Like an art dealer holding up a priceless painting, he pushed his right hand out in front of him. "It's this—your right wrist. If you learn to twist that throttle harder and more often, you'll burn everybody else on the track. And one more thing. This is the saying I've taken as my motto, so listen up: 'Winning isn't everything—it's *the only thing!*'"

Jeff looked around him, looked at faces, watched expressions. Everyone, it seemed was eating up the racing star's words as much as he was.

The first riding session was a kind of "show and tell" time, with Brent doing a lot of showing and very little telling. His pupils loved it. As they moved slowly from obstacle to obstacle around the course, they watched Brent work wonders on his highly tuned machine. They watched as he rounded the deep, sandy turn, dragging his handlebars and shooting a roostertail of sand thirty feet behind him. They watched him wheelie the length of the incredible uphill and fly skyward off the top.

"This guy is *stylish!*" said Ricky.

"Awesome is more like it," added Jeff.

"Pretty darn F—A—S—T!" said the MacAttack, in a poor imitation of Brent's own southern accent.

MacAttack turned to Adam for his opinion. "Tell us, Superman Bylow," he began, once again holding out an invisible microphone, "what do you think of Brent 'The Rage' Wade's fine riding style?"

Jeff was more interested in Adam's comment than he let on, so he listened closely.

Adam, spitting out the clover stem he had been chewing, looked almost angry. He leaned against his bike, not watching Brent anymore, and said in a serious tone, "We're not going to learn *anything* from this showoff!"

6

Shared Secrets

Racing camp flew by.

Each day was a flurry of theory classes, physical training, and riding sessions. The days were long—starting every morning at 5:45 for Jeff and Ricky with the Mind Power Option.

Darrel had convinced a few other riders to come, MacAttack among them, and the early morning session turned into a prestigious time for only those who were disciplined enough to rise at the crack of dawn. The sessions were short and powerful—Darrel read a verse from the Bible (to the surprise of the first-timers) and gave advice on mental preparation and the importance of a proper attitude.

On the third morning things got controversial. "I guess you remember what Brent said after I introduced him—maybe you even wrote it down. Well, let me say that I think he has the wrong attitude—winning *isn't* the only thing."

The "Mind Power Boys," as the early-risers came to be known, were split on the issue. Many, like Ricky, were at camp to learn how to beat everyone else, no matter what it took. Others, like MacAttack, agreed with Darrel that racing was worthwhile in other ways. Jeff rode the fence. *After all,* he said to himself, *isn't that what racing's all about, being number one?*

The riding sessions, without doubt the highpoint of each day, proved to be a study in contrasting styles. Darrel spent less time on his bike than the students and stood trackside pointing out the best lines through corners or emphasizing the importance of braking.

"There are only two speeds in motocross," he'd said, "full speed and full stop. You're either trying to accelerate fast as you can, or you're trying to stop as fast as you can."

He placed importance on being a "thinking racer." "Wild riders who throw lots of dirt, go highest off jumps, and hit the biggest bumps, may look fast—but only for the first few laps. If they don't crash out, then you can be sure they'll fade late in the race. Riding smoothly is not only safer, but it will help you conserve energy for a burst on the last lap. After all," and he smiled when he said this, "what are you out there for anyway? To win races or impress the girls?"

At this, Ricky leaned over to Jeff and gave him another vise-like squeeze on his arm, saying, "That's right, Tension, which *is* more important?"

Jeff was enjoying the week, more so each day. He particularly enjoyed the riding sessions that Brent conducted. He was a treat to watch.

"If you ever want to turn pro," Brent had said on the second day, "then this is how to do it." He rode up-track, turned around slowly, and aimed his bike at a three-hill section, a rough part of the course that had everyone puzzled. After revving his motor, he blasted toward the first hill like a two wheeled rocket. The bike came off it in top gear and soared over the next two hills, missing the last one by a hair's breadth and landing hard. He slowed, turned, and rode back to the group of students who whistled and clapped in approval.

Brent shut off his bike and concluded, "That, gentlemen, is how to get sponsors to notice you. Do something risky and create attention. I've taken a few rides in ambulances on the way to the top, but it's been worth it. Boring riders end up nobodies."

Jeff and the others ate up Brent's advice. Even the MacAttack was impressed. *Maybe*, Jeff thought, *I'll have a shot at the pros someday.* As each day passed, he became more and more fascinated with that idea.

The week raced on. The motocross students began to take on an air of superiority, began to feel like they were part of an extra-special club. The Thunder Ride facility had a lot to do with it. It was like an exclusive European training camp, set somewhere in the Alpine foothills, certainly somewhere quite different than dusty old Three Hills Raceway.

Jeff and his fellow racers overlooked things like the broken Coke machine—after all, they were beginning to drink fruit juices and eat granola, like Darrel. And they ignored the fact that there were no crowds watching them, because they enjoyed the special, secretive feel of the place.

They were growing into a tight-knit group. Even though they each knew that their on-track rivalries would continue, there was a growing comaraderie among them. In Jeff's eyes, this was great—at least mostly it was. He was beginning to like Ricky, and they spent a lot of time discussing racing. But he was concerned about his best friend MacAttack.

"Mac sure does spend a lot of time with Superman," Ricky said near the end of the week as they walked to the Mind Power Session.

"You mean Superdrip," Jeff replied in a sour voice. And it was then that he felt a jealousy like nothing else he'd ever felt. It had been bad enough that his favorite girl liked Adam—worse yet that his best friend did.

So it wasn't hard to understand why Jeff was tense the last evening at camp when MacAttack took him aside and said, "Adam and I are going to skip supper and go for a swim. Can you grab a couple of sandwiches for us to have later?"

Jeff frowned and replied in an unusual voice,

"What do you think I am, your servant boy?" And he walked off to the dining hall in a minor rage.

Ricky, at dinner, said, "Adam Bylow isn't so great. You know what I found out? He's more interested in nature photography than racing. You wouldn't believe it either. I asked him who he thought the best rider was—Darrel or Brent. Do you know what he said? He said 'Anybody that would do *this* for a living can't be very bright!' "

"He said that?" asked Jeff, puzzled.

"Yeah! And look at all the racing gear he's got! If anybody is gunning for a pro career, it's Bylow and he says he doesn't even like racing! He's nuts!"

"Either he's nuts or he's got a secret plan."

"Yeah, a secret plan to psych us all out. If anybody can play mind games, it's him. Can you believe it? Nature photography?"

Over at the swimming pool, as the long shadows of evening crept across the grass and onto the still, blue water, MacAttack sat talking with Superman Bylow.

They talked the way boys often do when they want to approach an important subject. They beat around the bush, made small-talk, gossiped about other riders, were both nervous.

Finally, the MacAttack went quiet and looked at Adam. The deserted poolside deck fell silent. Across the lawn they could hear chatter from the dining hall, and the dull electronic explosions from video games.

"What is it with you anyway, Adam?"

"What?"

"You know what I mean. Like, why are you so down on racing? If anybody has it made, you do. You're fast. You've got the right equipment. Your dad does everything for you."

"Oh, yea! Does he ever!"

"Something wrong with your dad?"

MacAttack's question hung heavy in the cool silence. Adam looked away to the left, then to the right, then spoke.

"My dad used to race The Mile. You know, at fairgrounds and places, the big races with modified Harleys. He never made it. He crashed a few times, and when you crash in that kind of a race, you don't just shrug it off and jump back on. He's got a pin in his hip."

"Okay. So what?"

"Well, he's always saying that he blew it—a chance at the pros—because he didn't have the support to do it right. So he's making sure *I* don't blow it."

"That's great, isn't it?"

"He goes too far, though! I mean—he plans a year in advance what races he'll take me to. He takes his holidays to coincide with racing camps and state championships, and practically *forces* me to race. If I don't win, he gets on my case and says, 'Look at the money I've put into your racing! Look at what I've done for you—and you didn't win!' He gets mad, and pushes me even harder."

"What about your mom?"

"I hardly ever see her. They were divorced two years ago. With all my racing, I don't get time to visit her. And she hates racing."

"So what are you going to do?"

"I'm going to fake sick at the amateur championship next week at Charger Stadium. I'm not going to ride. *That* will *really* get to him!"

The two boys sat quietly, both thinking. Their thoughts, had they known it, were strangely parallel.

"It's weird," said MacAttack, "but we've both got father problems. I don't usually say anything about this, but if you'll keep it quiet, I'll tell you."

Adam nodded.

"I guess my dad's pretty close to being an alcoholic. Maybe not quite, but close. If I was on the brink of winning the National Motocross championship, he wouldn't even come to the race—he'd just sit in his big armchair, drink beer, and watch baseball. He couldn't care beans about what I do, especially racing."

MacAttack went on to explain his problems to Adam and the words came out painfully. He hadn't even told Jeff some of the things he told Adam that evening at the pool.

Adam asked an unexpected question: "Doesn't believing in God help you?"

"God helps me with the problems, but God never promised to take all our problems away. He sure hasn't taken mine away."

"Or mine," said Adam, and the two racers smiled, feeling somehow happy that they'd talked.

Later that evening, while watching videos in the dining hall, Jeff pulled up a chair beside MacAttack.

"Sorry for sounding angry when you asked me for that sandwich."

"No problem."

"But what is it with you and Superman? I thought we came to this camp to learn how to beat him."

"We did. But is it against the law to make friends with our competitors?"

"No. But it should be. Anyway, tomorrow's the last day of camp and I'm going to call my dad to find out when he'll get here to pick us up. Do you think we'll be packed by 4:00?"

"Easy. You know, you're lucky to have a dad like that."

"Lucky? My dad's not so great. He hasn't been to see one of my races yet this year."

Jeff felt a twinge of guilt having said this, knowing that MacAttack's father had *never* been to one of his races. But then he thought of Adam's dad and said, "I mean, look at Mr. Bylow. He does *everything* for his son. If only my dad was like that when it comes to racing!"

Another video started. It was a tape of the Los Angeles Coliseum Supercross.

"We saw this on TV last spring, remember?" said Jeff, excitedly. "Brent's in it! He pulls off a second!"

It felt good to be able to call Brent Wade by his first name, and it was great to know that the rider they watched on the videotape was teaching at their camp.

The excitement of the video race overcame thoughts of fathers, and problems. Most of the cheering boys who sat in the dimmed dining hall were ready to admit that they were sad school would finish the next day.

MacAttack stood and walked up to the TV set.

"Here it comes," he said, finger on the 'pause' button. The film rolled on and when Brent Wade flew from the big jump, doing a one-handed "peace sign" jump, MacAttack hit the button and Brent froze, mid-air. Then the picture went into rewind and the boys broke up as MacAttack rewound, played, rewound and played the famous one-handed jump shot in quick succession. "Remember what Brent said about getting sponsors to notice you? He's the only guy I know who can jump backwards with one hand!"

Jeff and the others were overcome with laughter. MacAttack had, over the course of the week, gained a firm hold on the title of "Camp Clown." Adam however, didn't join in on the fun. When the video rolled forward again, into the heat of the stadium race, he rose quietly and left the room.

No one, not even his new friend, the Camp Clown, noticed he'd gone.

7
Closing Day

The last day of camp dawned cool and rainy.

Fitting weather, thought Jeff, as he jumped from the top bunk and threw a pair of goggles at a groggy Ricky Jackson.

"Breakfast time, racing star. Without the Mind Power Option you've had more than enough sleep."

"Oh sure," said Ricky, through a haze that seemed thicker than the rain clouds outside. "Sleeping until 6 a.m. is really sleeping in!"

The morning footrace, which had become a camp tradition, was a sloppy affair, but Jeff loved it. Not only did the rain keep him cool, but he was proud of the progress he'd made over the short five days. He was hardly out of breath when he crossed the finish line, shoes caked with mud. And he was in the top five, right behind Adam Bylow.

Things only improved. At an informal "awards" ceremony following lunch, Jeff received one of the coveted passes that would allow him onto the field and into the pro pit area at the Charger Stadium Supercross. He, MacAttack, Ricky, Adam and the two Baysville Crazies were all chosen because of their progress during the week.

Jeff and MacAttack gave each other the "thumbs up" at this news. Even Adam seemed pleased.

The last riding session, however, was a minor disaster. Usually, it was a time to demonstrate all that you'd learned, being matched with riders of equal skill, but the rains turned the session into a comical farce.

Adam, matched with Ricky for a one lap dual, got stuck in a mudhole that was swollen from heavy rain. Ricky, in an attempt to find a dry line through the same trouble spot, clipped a course marker and ended up face down in the thick, gooey mud.

Darrel and Brent, watching from trackside, could hardly balance their bikes for laughter. Darrel waved his arms for attention and yelled, "And *that* gentlemen, is how *not* to do it!" He laughed hard, then talked quietly with Brent for a moment.

"Brent will demonstrate how it's done in the big leagues," Darrel said fastening his helmet strap.

Brent revved his Honda and dropped the clutch, showering MacAttack and the Baysville Crazies with fine mud, much to the delight of the other spattered riders.

He rode up-track and turned, aiming at the tricky bog which rested like a giant puddle at the lowest part of the course.

He'd done this a hundred times, after all—he was a pro. His strategy became obvious as he rode the downhill slope, gaining terrific speed.

"This will be deadly!" said MacAttack, grinning with anticipation.

Brent's plan was to gain as much speed as possible and hit the large whoop-dee-doo that everyone else had avoided as they concentrated on the coming mud. He'd jump the deepest mud and land on the far side, hopefully on solid ground.

But even pros make mistakes.

At the last instant, before take-off, his rear wheel caught a greasy rut, throwing him sideways. There were no one-handed peace signs this time, only a professional nose dive into the bog just left of the mired-down Adam.

So went the remainder of the riding session. The rain was so heavy and the mud so deep that riding some sections of the raceway became impossible. Stalled motocross bikes lined the ruts and leaned on the track side fences. Only Darrel and the Baysville Crazies made it through the Mud Gulley and that with some great difficulty.

The inevitable happened. Jeff, watching MacAttack's eyes, smiled and questioned quietly, "Pool Wars?"

"Not quite," said the brown, goo-covered clown. He thrust his fist skyward and proclaimed at his loudest "MUD WARS!" Then he ran and dived headlong into the mudhole. He was soon joined by a dozen others and the mud-wrestling tournament began.

Mid-afternoon, after some serious shower-sessions had ended, the school met for the last time, dried off and tired, in the shelter of the dining hall.

Outside, the rain continued, harder than ever. Jeff could see some parents arriving already, but he didn't see the Jamestown Swat Van.

Darrel Boyd gave out certificates to each of the 52 riders, commenting on each as he called them, using nicknames wherever possible.

"Randy, the MacAttack, the man who ate five Thunderburgers at one sitting and lived to tell about it. . . ."

"Jim Thomas, Bayesville Crazy, the only racer crazy enough to do a belly flop off the diving board in full racing gear, helmet, goggles, boots and all. . . ."

Jeff braced for the unknown as his turn came up. *What can he say about me?*

"Tension Scott, the only rider brave enough to wear a sign on his back that says 'I'd die for Charlene'! "

Jeff went pale and his heart skipped a beat. Then he turned flaming red and reached behind him. He tore the paper from his back.

"Where did this come from?" he blurted out, almost drowned by the laughter around him. Ricky and MacAttack, sitting on each side of him, smiled

69

straight ahead and gave both of his arms vise-like squeezes.

He smiled too. "It's not *me* who'll die!" he said. Then he joined in the laughter.

Darrel called for quiet and began to talk about racing strategy. He concluded by saying, "And some of you guys, about fifteen yesterday, have been coming out to the Mind Power Option every morning. You fellows have been discussing one of the most important aspects of racing that I know about—attitude. I think it's safe to say that mental attitude has a lot to do with winning or losing. And it has even more to do with whether we enjoy racing."

"When you're in an atmosphere like this—lots of competition, great instruction," and he nodded to Brent as he said it, "it's pretty easy to get obsessed with excitement and the chance to succeed.

"Excitement and success are okay. Don't get me wrong. But racing's a lot like life. If we start out in a flurry of energy, thinking only about what *we* can accomplish, with championship in mind, well you know what will happen. Before long, racing won't be so much fun anymore. Pretty soon it will be work, and hard work at that. The only joy will be in winning yet a bigger race, and then a bigger one. You might even get to the point where you feel like your biggest goal is to beat the other guy no matter what it takes—running him off the track, ramming him, cheating, whatever. At that point, motocross ceases to be the fun sport it should be.

"My advice to you guys is to enjoy motocross as good healthy fun, first. The winning will come later or maybe it won't but you'll last longer and be further ahead in the end."

Jeff watched MacAttack's reaction and felt a little like judging him and saying, "You've been right all along, you nut!" but he didn't.

But it's true, he thought. *Randy knows how to have fun while he's racing. I guess he knows how to have fun living, period.*

Yet Jeff felt a twinge of resentment that was stronger than he realized, a resentment towards MacAttack's new friendship with Adam. *I don't know why he likes Adam,* Jeff thought. *All Adam wants to do is win, win, win. He doesn't enjoy racing at all.*

Brent took the platform. "I've got Team Honda jerseys for everybody out in my van afterwards and I've autographed them all."

"Excellent!" whispered Ricky to Jeff.

Then Brent made his closing speech talking about the problems of being a pro rider and what the boys could expect if they wanted to go far.

"Like Darrel says, you have to enjoy the sport if you want to succeed. But even more important, you have to want to succeed. You can have as much fun as you want and still stay in the bush leagues."

"To be a pro you have to take chances, and ride on the ragged edge. To go National you have to be ready to battle it out tooth and nail. In one of *your* races, there might be two or three guys that can

71

win. In one of mine, all thirty riders are capable. It's that close."

The dining hall was silent. Jeff remembered a preacher that had spoken at Jamestown Community Church once. Except for that time, he'd never seen a crowd so attentive.

"The Mr. Nice Guys do not usually get the top spot. If you aren't willing to dive inside and steal a line from the next guy, forget it. You've got to be so hungry for the win that you can taste it. Be nice off the track and be a good salesman for your sponsors, but on the track, do what is necessary."

"Say it with me," said Brent and he had the riders repeat out loud his slogan for the week, "Winning isn't everything, it's *the only thing*."

"Do you believe it?"

A shout went up, "Ya!"

But Jeff didn't shout, nor did MacAttack or Adam.

Ricky didn't shout either. Rather he wore a determined grin and set his eyes on Brent Wade.

"This guy knows what it's all about!" he said quietly.

"Pretty sure of himself, anyway."

"It will be wild next weekend, watching our two instructors battle it out in the pro race. . . ."

"Yea, and then us the next day in the amatuer race!"

"On the same track!"

Jeff and Ricky grinned at each other.

"You know how he said 'Hungry to win,' Jeff?

Well, I feel pretty starved for this win at the stadium next Saturday!"

Ricky was no exception. More than a dozen of the boys at the racing camp were registered to race in the Amateur 80A class at the stadium the next week and they were all "hungry." A win there would mean a position on the starting line at the Amateur Nationals. And who knew where that might lead?

Jeff had never ridden on a Stadium Supercross track before, nor had any of his friends. He'd heard that Adam had, out in California, and finished poorly.

How many hours had he spent daydreaming about sailing high off of that big jump, the roar of 30,000 fans louder than his screaming engine. And Charlene would be waiting for him at the finish line, waiting with a victory kiss, and. . . .

MacAttack ended the daydream.

"Tension, I'm going over to Adam's motorhome. He's going to show me some photos of Big Sur."

"Sir who?"

"Big Sur! It's a section of the California coastline with big cliffs and lots of trees and birds and surf and stuff. They camped there last summer after the races at Oakland. Wanna come and see them? You're invited."

"Look, Randy," Jeff said, knowing it would be no friendly 'yes' he was about to give, for he never called his friend Randy—always MacAttack, Mac or Bozo. "We better pack our stuff. My dad should be here with the van pretty soon."

"I'm packed."

"Your bike, too?"

"Ready to go."

"Did you get your Honda jersey from Brent?"

"Don't want one—don't ride a Honda!"

MacAttack smiled widely and added an interesting suggestion, "Why don't you get mine? Then you'll have two Honda jerseys. One for you and one for Charlene!"

"Oh sure!" said Jeff, once again embarrassed, remembering the sign he'd worn on his back. He wasn't sure why he was embarrassed though. After all, Charlene would love a Honda shirt and besides, she was certainly not the sort of girl to be embarrassed about. She was gorgeous!

"Come over to the motorhome and get me when your dad arrives," said MacAttack as he rose to leave, "or come with me now. Adam's a great photographer. He's got Nikon equipment worth over five hundred bucks!"

He's great! . . . He's got nice equipment. That's all I ever hear about that guy, thought Jeff.

He left the dining hall and went to pack.

Saying goodbye to racing school buddies wasn't all that hard. Jeff would see most of them soon at another race. But it *was* a bit difficult to pack and leave Thunder Ridge.

His dad arrived, but in Mr. Brenner's Jamestown Honda van this time.

"Sorry, but if ever the force needs the SWAT van it's Saturday nights!"

74

MacAttack had seen the van arrive and after saying goodbye to Adam and his dad, he ran over to Jeff, beaming.

"Must have been good photos," said Jeff.

"They were, but guess what?"

"What?"

"No, guess!"

"Adam's sold his motorcycles to help the Wildlife Fund?"

"No! Adam and his dad are heading back to Jamestown to camp at Riley Lake again. I asked him to come along to church tomorrow morning!"

"What?"

"I told him about Ben Masters. Isn't that great?"

Silence. Jeff couldn't believe it. Charlene would be at church for sure. He didn't want *her* to meet Adam.

"Jeff—aren't we supposed to ask our friends to come to church and learn about God?"

Jeff turned and walked quickly back to his dorm, saying nothing.

Ricky was packing when Jeff entered.

"You look steamed!" Ricky said.

"Superman Super Jerk again!"

"Want to do him in at the Supercross!"

"We don't have a chance of beating that guy, Rick."

"We do if we follow my plan. It will be risky, but like Brent says, it'll be worth it. Can I count you in? Top secret stuff."

Jeff felt a tearing inside—a tearing away from his

best friend and the kind of person he knew he should be. He knew he was making a mistake, conspiring with Ricky, being angry at MacAttack, sulking like a little kid.

"I'm in!" he said as the tearing feeling grew. "Tell me your plan."

8
Hidden Revenge

Jeff sat silently at the rear of Jamestown Community Church. He had much to think about and he rehearsed the topics in his mind—Ricky's secret plan to beat Adam at the amateur Supercross, MacAttack's friendship with Adam, and Adam coming to church.

The last point was of immediate concern. If Adam accepted MacAttack's invitation and came to the morning service, he'd meet Charlene for sure.

Jeff had chosen a spot near one of the rear doors, hoping to head off Charlene before she could meet Adam. He saw Ben Masters and watched as he talked with some of the little kids sitting near the front.

He remembered Ben's talk at the pool party about authority and he remembered the dirt bike they'd heard at the quarry pit that night. How wrong they'd all been about the identify of the "mystery rider!" Even he hadn't suspected the truth.

Jeff watched Ben's easy smile and happy manner. *I wonder if he knows what's really going on here?* he thought. *Likely not.* After all, how could somebody as old as Ben take motocross or young love seriously!

Then Jeff's heart skipped a beat and the lump that usually came to his throat returned, bigger and lumpier than ever. He saw Charlene, Sherry and Linda sit down far on the other side of the auditorium.

A minute later, he saw MacAttack (in a "Steelers" jersey) and Art slide into the row with them.

No Adam. Jeff smiled triumphantly and rose to walk over and join his friends.

Just then his dad approached him. "Jeff, maybe you can help. A friend of yours and Randy's is here. He's looking for Randy." As he spoke, Adam walked in, looking unaccustomed to a church building.

"Maybe you can show Adam where Randy's sitting."

"Hi, Adam."

"Hi, Jeff."

This is a disaster! thought Jeff and he felt the palms of his hands go clammy. *Not only does my main rival show up at my church, but I have to introduce him to Charlene!*

"They're over here," Jeff said with words like ice, and he added coldly, "nice you could make it."

They walked over to where Charlene and the

78

others sat. Jeff tapped MacAttack on the shoulder and said no more.

MacAttack stood, took a low bow and introduced Adam to his friends in the voice of a smooth Frenchman.

Jeff couldn't take it. He turned and left, unnoticed in the flurry of dramatic introductions.

This is no place to be angry, he thought, as he walked briskly to the back of the church, *but I'm angry anyway!*

He brushed past Ben Masters without a "hello." He had his jacket on and his mind made up by the time he reached the foyer.

His dad saw him.

"Jeff," he called, in a tone that meant "come here now."

Jeff replied, "Dad, I really shouldn't have come to church this morning. I mean, I've had a long week and I'm bushed." He hesitated. As he considered his next statement he felt the same kind of tearing inside he'd felt talking with Ricky the day before, but he closed his mind to it and continued, "I really feel sick, I'm just going to go home and lay down for a while, maybe go for a walk. I'll see you and mom after lunch, okay?"

"Want me to drive you home, son?"

"No, the service is about to start. I'll be okay. I'll just walk slowly."

Jeff walked out of the Jamestown Community Church, looking ill. He rounded the bend at the corner of the lawn and turned behind the tall cedar fence that lined the parking lot. He broke into a run.

Why wait? he was thinking. *I told Ricky I'd meet him after the service, but he's probably already there.* His mind raced in time with his flying feet. A week of training at racing camp had paid off. He was home in no time flat.

Quickly, he donned his riding gear and wheeled his Honda from the garage. He pushed it down the sidewalk, running alongside, sweating inside his helmet. He jumped and rode side saddle down the long hill at the edge of his neighborhood, not daring to start the engine. Then he turned onto a well-worn path that led through a weedy field. There, he started his bike. He rode the path uphill, as fast as he could, feeling a soreness in his arms that came from the last week's work, but sensing a new confidence and speed.

He crested the hill and could see Ben Master's house about a quarter mile away. Then he rode up to a derelict chain-link fence, slipped through a hole in it's side, and shut off his engine. He was in the old quarry pit.

Jeff had stopped to listen for Ricky's engine, but instead he heard the words of Ben Masters, coming back again and again, ". . . it all boils down to a lack of respect for authority . . . man's authority . . . God's authority."

"Oh, this is stupid!" he said out loud as he considered his predicament. Not only had he skipped church to come and ride at the quarry pit when it was off limits, but he'd lied to his dad about it all. "He'll *kill* me!" he said even louder. A cold sweat broke out on the back of his neck. He felt as though he was being watched. He wished he was back at the church.

Just then an 80cc Yamaha came to life far on the other side of the cavernous pit. Jeff started his Honda and rode toward it.

Despite the battle that raged inside, he had set the ball rolling and wasn't going to back down now. He and Ricky put their secret plan of action into effect.

It was not too brilliant, in all honesty, and the more Jeff thought about it, the less confident he became. But he was determined to try anything if it meant he could beat Adam Bylow at the amateur Supercross.

The plan was simple—to spend as much time practicing at the old quarry pit as possible, even when the place was strictly off limits. Part two of the plan was to practice jumping a supercross-style double-jump and have it "wired" by race day.

"Brent was telling some of us at camp what the supercross track will be like, how big the jumps will be and all that," said Ricky, sweating and dusty. "So I've been working all morning building this set of doubles to be about the right distance apart."

Jeff looked at the forty-foot gap between the two small ramps.

"This is insane."

"Well, Brent said that's the way they build them on a Supercross track. He said top speed in fifth gear on an 80cc bike should clear it."

"Really?" Jeff just stared at the jump.

"Really! But where have *you* been all this time?"

"At church."

"Did Superman show up with Mac?"

"Yeah!"

"Meet Charlene?"

"Of course!"

"Well, what are we waiting for?"

Ricky started his Yamaha and let it idle. He wiped his dusty goggles with the cuff of his jersey and fastened them in place. Then he rode off to find an approach to the first ramp.

As Jeff sat and watched, his mind swirled with a hundred thoughts. Ricky, he realized, had become a much closer friend over the past week. Jeff knew their friendship could be a really good one if it developed away from the crazy hassles of racing. But what had pulled them together so far? A mutual hatred of Adam and a scheme that put them both in a bad position. They were trespassing—they were breaking the law.

Yet Jeff admired Ricky for his main attribute: *He's a fighter*, he thought. *I'll bet he'll even clear this insane jump.*

As Jeff watched Ricky run up through the gears on approach to the first ramp, he realized his friend had no choice—he *had* to clear the double-jump, or he'd be in big trouble. If his front wheel hit the lip of the second ramp, he could be hurt bad.

The screaming Yamaha rocketed into the air and

Jeff could see Ricky's expression as he flew by, wide-eyed and terrified.

With only inches to spare, Ricky landed on the down slope of the second ramp. His Yamaha's suspension bottomed out so the landing was anything but smooth. But he'd done it! He wobbled, kicked a leg out for balance, then straightened up. Jeff could hear his whoop of triumph above the Yamaha engine.

"No problem, Jeffrey!" said Ricky, pulling alongside. "The secret, like Brent says, is right here," and he held up his throttle hand. "When in doubt—gas it!"

Jeff looked around at the vast old pit—mounds of gravel, well-worn trails, smaller jumps and hills. "I think I'll just practice corners for a while, then try it."

"You've got cold feet!"

"I do not!"

"You're gun shy!"

"I am not!"

"Then try the jump! Do it for Charlene! No—better yet—do it for Superman Bylow!"

Jeff's knuckles, hidden inside his gloves, were turning white as he squeezed the grips on his Honda. Charlene. Adam. As *he* sat on his bike, *they* were sitting in church. Maybe even side by side.

Jeff tightened the strap on his Bell helmet and kicked his Honda to life.

"What gear did you use?" he yelled at Ricky.

"Tapped out in sixth!"

Jeff swung around and rode quickly to the same place that Ricky had used for a launching pad. He looked down the fifty yard straight. He revved his engine.

This is crazy, he thought.

Charlene came back to his mind, and Adam, high over a jump in the coliseum. . . .

He revved his engine again.

Slipping his bike into gear, he looked at Ricky sitting by the first jump.

What's he doing?

Ricky was waving and pointing, frantically.

Somebody riding up the other side of the jump or something?

But Ricky was pointing to a place *behind* Jeff. Jeff turned around.

Parked by the hole in the fence where he'd come into the pit was a black and white car. "Jamestown Police Force" it said on the side.

9
The Truth Comes Out

Jeff's earlier lie about feeling ill was no longer a falsehood. His stomach felt queasy; a cold sweat broke out on his forehead.

Two officers walked toward him and he recognized both of them. One, in uniform, was Sergeant MacDonald, his dad's boss. The other, in a brown suit, was his dad.

He looked back and forth, from his dad to Sergeant MacDonald to Ricky, who sat still by the jump, knowing there was no place to run.

Jeff expected his dad to speak first and speak angrily. Instead, he stood silently beside Sergeant MacDonald and said nothing.

Sergeant MacDonald did the talking. "We received a call at the station from a neighbor, saying there were some trespassers in the quarry. I paged your father at church because he had told me before that if this happened, he'd like to personally go and talk to the culprits. He told me that he wanted to stop the trespassing riders from ruining it for responsible riders like his son. What do you have to say about *that*, Jeff?"

Jeff was silent. Sergeant MacDonald carried on.

"You know, of course, that no riders are allowed to use this property on a Sunday morning. Town Council decided that last year. You know that you're trespassing, Jeff."

Jeff couldn't look up. *Why didn't I stay in church?*

"I think the best thing for me to do is to leave you two fellows here with your dad. You've done the damage, though. Town Council will likely lock the gates for good. I suppose I'll have to recommend it."

Sergeant MacDonald whistled and motioned for Ricky to join them. Ricky did so. Sergeant MacDonald was a big, bold man in his uniform. People tended to obey him. He walked back to the police cruiser and drove off leaving Jeff and Ricky with Mr. Scott.

A terrible silence filled the cavernous quarry pit. Jeff could hear boats on Riley Lake and cars winding up the hill past Ben Master's place.

"Well!" said his dad finally.

Jeff and Ricky looked at each other, then back at their boots. Jeff kicked the sand.

"You don't understand, dad," he said at last.

86

"Understand what?"

"Why we're here; why I skipped church."

"And why you lied to me, and why you're both trespassing?" Mr. Scott was angry. Jeff could tell by the tone of his voice that they would get nowhere now. He also knew what would happen next.

"Both of you realize that your inconsideration will cost all of the riders in Jamestown a place to ride. This is definitely not the way to make friends."

Although he was addressing both of them, he was staring at Jeff only. The double role of policemen and father was not easy for him.

His dad said, "I'll be calling your parents, Ricky. They'll want to know about this. Push your bike home and don't start it. Push it. Now!"

As they watched Ricky go, Jeff realized he still had his helmet and gloves on. He took them off quickly and tried to comb his hair with his fingers as if neatness would take the edge off his dad's scolding.

Jeff could see the inevitable coming. He could hear his dad, any minute now, saying, "No more motocross for you," and he could see himself grounded for weeks. He wouldn't get to the Charger Stadium Supercross and his field pass would be wasted. Everybody would find out and Charlene would think he was a real jerk.

Jeff felt like crying, but wouldn't let himself. After all, he was a motocross racer, and almost old enough to drive a car, and besides, his dad never cried.

Mr. Scott sat down on the sandy ground where it started to slope up and out of the Quarry Pit.

"Come and sit down, Jeff."

Here it comes, thought Jeff, tensing for the worst.

"Son, of course I'm disappointed in you. You know that."

"Yeah."

"MacDonald could put you in hot water, but I think you'll both get off with a stiff warning. But that's just part of it."

Jeff's dad picked up a handful of sand and sifted it slowly through his fingers.

"I've sensed a real battle going on inside you, and you've been a changed boy these last three weeks. I didn't really put it together until today when that Adam boy came into church. Then I found you out here with Ricky. . . ."

His dad related his theory on Jeff's inner turmoil. He told Jeff he thought it had something to do with how little attention he had been giving to him. He said he wished he could get to more races and was going to try hard to do so.

"You know Jeff, I was angry when MacDonald picked me up at church today. I said to him, 'Jim,' I said, 'whoever it is that's riding up there should have his bike confiscated. I don't care if it's the mayor's son. I don't want my son's practice area closed down because of somebody else's foolishness.' "

Jeff felt a tear on his cheek.

"But when I saw it was you, my tune changed. I feel partly responsible."

"You're not, dad."

"I think I am."

"Well, you're not."

And they had the first good talk they'd had in months. Jeff told his dad all about how he almost hated Adam and how he cared for Charlene and how he was losing his trust in MacAttack. His dad talked about the pressures of policework—how he often felt like quitting, how it all worried Mrs. Scott, and how it sometimes made him blind to his son's needs.

"Jeffrey, look at the time! Your mother will hang us! We've missed lunch and she was doing Escargots today."

"Snails?"

"Well, at least they're different."

"I'm *glad* we missed lunch!"

They walked home, taking turns pushing the Honda. Jeff looked at his dad, bent over and sweating in his brown Sunday suit, pushing the bike. *What a dad*, he thought, for the first time in ages.

The week that followed was not an easy one. The Town Council voted to lock the quarry pit until something could be decided properly. Jeff and Ricky took flak from some of the other riders and had to go to the station for a lecture by Sergeant MacDonald.

But all that faded quickly as the big Supercross weekend approached. On Thursday night, the day before the trip to the city, Jeff, MacAttack and Art sat outside the Burger Monster.

MacAttack was trying to eat a Monster Burger and balance his BMX bike at the same time.

Art said, "That was sure some big scheme you and Ricky concocted, Jeff."

"Brilliant my dear Watson," said MacAttack, taking a bite and wobbling badly.

"Let's change the subject. So tell me Mac, did Adam like church on Sunday?"

MacAttack took his last mouthful, swallowed and toppled sideways, onto the grass. As he got up he said, "I guess so. He seemed to. Charlene invited him to every party from now until 2001!"

Art nudged Jeff. "Look out," he whispered and pointed. Sherry, Linda and Charlene rode up on their bikes.

Sherry and Linda were far more interested in watching MacAttack balance his stationery bike than they were in eating.

"I can do both," said MacAttack, charming Linda's milkshake from her.

Charlene sat down on the red picnic table beside Jeff. "How are you, Mr. Racer?" she said.

Jeff was suspicious. "Fine. And how are you Miss Social Convenor," he said as he felt good about being able to come back with a smooth line.

"I met Adam at church. He's a real nice guy."

"He is," said Jeff with about as much conviction as a dead snail.

"He told me that you are going to be at the Supercross tomorrow night and that you won a field pass."

"Yeah."

"And that you're going to be in the amateur race Saturday morning."

"Yeah."

"Aren't you excited? I am!" Charlene said earnestly.

Why is she so excited? wondered Jeff. *It won't be televised up here.*

"I'm excited because I'm going too! My brother's boss gave him tickets and he's taking me. We're going to stay over at my aunt's and then come to your race Saturday! *That's* why I'm excited! I can be your cheering section!"

"Mine?" Jeff was a living, blushing, goose-bump.

"Well, yours and MacAttack's and Adam's."

Jeff could see Art, behind Charlene. He was making faces and squeezing his arm. Jeff laughed and asked Charlene if she'd like a Coke.

"Our cheerleader needs her pay," he said, smiling at her and wondering.

Later, he and MacAttack rode with Art back to Mr. Brenner's shop. The big mean "Jamestown Honda" sign cast a reddish glow on the sidewalk, but the "Closed" sign hung in the front door.

They went around back and in through the service entrance. Mr. Brenner was already hard at work on Jeff's and Randy's bikes.

"I've tuned them. Now you Superstars can clean them. These little babies have got a big day on Saturday." He slapped the blue seat on Jeff's Honda as he said it.

Two hours later, Jeff and MacAttack quietly rode home on their BMX bikes, having cleaned and loaded their racers into Mr. Brenner's van.

"Art's dad's pretty good to help us out like this," said MacAttack.

"We're almost as lucky as Adam," said Jeff, probing his friend, trying for a reaction.

He got one.

"I wish you'd lay off Adam!" said MacAttack.

"What's eating you?"

"Look, Jeff, you're always going on about 'Adam the Jerk this' or 'Superman Bylow that.' You really aren't clued in, are you?"

Jeff stopped his bike and looked his friend in the eye. This was the confrontation he'd wanted.

"No, *you* look Mac. You and I used to be best friends. Now all you talk about is Adam, Adam, Adam, and you almost talk like he has it hard or something! I mean, look at him. He's got it made!"

MacAttack shook his head and frowned. "You don't understand, do you?"

"No, I don't! And why do you have to bring him to *our* church? Charlene's practically *crazy* about him!"

The MacAttack, exhibiting that rare side of himself few ever saw, swung off his bike, sat down on the curb and talked quietly to Jeff. It was *Randy* speaking now.

"Adam has it harder than *anybody* realizes. If he had his way, he'd never go to another motocross race again."

"What?"

"Let me explain."

And he did. He told Jeff about Mr. Bylow's obsession with winning, about the pressure on Adam to do nothing but the best, about the heavy racing schedule Tunesmith racing kept, about Adam's love for photography.

"Are you putting me on?" Jeff wanted to be skeptical. He wanted to hold onto his belief that Adam was an egotistical win-hungry racer. Yet, despite this, he couldn't quite bring himself to doubt Randy.

"It's the truth, Jeff. And if you promise not to tell, I'll show you how bad it really is with Adam."

"I promise."

"For sure?"

"For sure."

"Okay. Well, you know his dad looks at the Amateur Supercross as the big step in Adam's climb to the pros. Adam's going to pull out just before the start and fake illness. He figures his dad will be so upset he'll call off the rest of the season and go home."

Jeff didn't know whether to smile or frown.

"That will be good news for us, won't it?" he said hesitantly.

"Not really. The racing bigshots are already scouting Adam. Reps from some of the factory teams will be there, and if Adam isn't in *our* race, they probably won't even watch it. It's like being in the World Series knowing that the best team didn't even show up. It'll be an anti-climax."

Jeff was silent and thoughtful. He and Randy rode home and separated; he to the brick house with the police cruiser in front, Randy down the hill to the place where even now his father would be stretched out in front of the TV, asleep.

"Bike's all race-prepped?" said Jeff's dad from the kitchen.

"Ready for battle, dad!"

"Your mom and I are working on cleaning your racing outfit. Next time pick a clean sport—like mud wrestling or something!"

In bed, Jeff lay awake, fitfully turning over and over. Mentally, he went through the motions of starting the race in Charger Stadium, and he thought about MacAttack and Adam. A twinge of guilt tore at him from the inside. He felt an urge to say "I'm sorry, Adam" and to try to help his competitor enjoy racing. Then his mind went back to the race. As sleep finally set in, he once again saw Ricky flying high over the monstrous double jump at the Old Quarry Pit. This was the jump he would face Saturday morning, the one he hadn't tried. And he remembered Ricky's look of wide-eyed terror. . . .

10

Supercross at Charger Stadium

Friday morning dawned hot and sunny. Heat waves rose, shimmering, from the black pavement that carried the boys toward the city and, when the first sky-scraping buildings rose on the horizon, they waved and bent, their distant images distorted by the heat.

They travelled in a mini-convoy of two vans. Art and Mr. Brenner led the way in the "Jamestown Honda" van, transporting the precious cargo of motocross bikes and tools. Mr. Scott drove the second, the Jamestown SWAT van which was once again freed from duty. Jeff was feeling pretty good about things. His dad had come through after all, taking the day off to get them to the race—the biggest race any of them had entered.

"And *we think* we're off to a supercross," joked MacAttack, looking back at Ricky and Jeff from the front passenger's seat. "Really, we're off to serve another 10-15 in the State Pen."

"Motorcycle gangsters!" said Mr. Scott.

"Burger killers!" said Mac.

They closed in rapidly on the shimmering skyline. As they passed acres of low factories, they were slowed by heavier traffic. Then they caught the expressway that led along the river to Charger Stadium. The stadium was at once both larger and smaller than they'd imagined.

"Why is it so low?" asked Ricky.

"It's dug five stories down into the ground," answered Jeff's dad, a football fan who'd been to the stadium before.

They parked their vans in "E-8," the section of the parking lot reserved for entrants to Saturday's amateur race. Then they registered for the next days event. They did it wide-eyed and quiet, as if signing on to serve in some majestic undertaking.

They were all glad, a minute later, to spot Darrel Boyd. He waved and approached. The very sight of him gave confidence to Jeff and his friends.

"Gentlemen, your field passes," he said, bowing and handing each of the boys an orange card marked "Press/Photo" and a plastic holder to keep it in.

"Want to come in and see the track being constructed?"

Darrel took the three riders around the side of the stadium and down into the press tunnel.

"Just show the security guard your pass when you go in. In fact, if you act naturally, like you've done this lots of times before, he won't even look at your pass. Act like you know what you're doing." Darrel stopped, looked at the boys and furrowed his brow, "On second thought, forget what I said and just follow me."

They walked through two sets of revolving doors which whistled and shuddered with the great air pressure of the dome.

"This place is pumped up like a balloon; that's how the roof stays up," explained Darrel.

The security guard, eating a chocolate donut and reading a football magazine, didn't even look up as they entered. "Motocross press on level 3," he said from behind his magazine.

"X-ray eyes!" whispered Mac to Jeff.

Off the elevator, Darrel led them down a narrow corridor, spic and span, lined with football posters and schedules. They walked past doors marked "NBC Sports," "Scoreboard," and "Radio Press-room."

Through a glass window in one of the doors, Jeff spotted a view that stopped him dead in his tracks.

It was only a peephole view, but it was terrific. Far below, he could see a corner of the field, and thousands of empty, blue seats. A bulldozer drove slowly through his field of vision, over one artificial hill into a forty-foot valley and up another hill.

"Ricky!" Jeff called, as if he was having a heart-attack. "Check it out! It's the double jump!"

But Darrel, Ricky and Mac, further down the hall, turned and went into one of the large press boxes. Jeff ran and joined them.

Only a few people had arrived in the press box and they sat behind long desks, studying the entry sheets of the orders. One man surveyed the track with binoculars. Another radioed instructions to a worker on the field.

"Way over at the end, Rick!" said Jeff.

"It's my double-jump!"

"That's right, but it's even bigger than the one you jumped in the quarry pit!"

Ricky didn't reply—only stared.

"This is *unbelievable!*" explained MacAttack, drinking in the immensity of the cavernous stadium. "How many people, Darrel?"

"It seats 70,000. Maybe 60,000 tonight."

"That's everybody in Jamestown plus a friend each!"

Jeff sat in the front row of the press box and ran his finger down the rider entry sheet. Brent Wade was listed in the top ten, in good position for a strong finish at the seasons end. A win at Charger Stadim would boost him into fifth or sixth overall depending on the finishes of the other riders.

Jeff looked for Darrel's name and position and his finger travelled down two columns of names before he found it. Darrel sat in thirty-eighth spot, well out of the hunt for any sort of championship position.

As if reading his mind, Darrel walked over and said, "You're lucky to even find my name in there.

98

I've missed three west coast races this season, so I'm glad just to have a few points. Travel is expensive."

You don't have to apologize, Jeff thought. He realized that winning *was* important to Darrel. He wondered how badly Darrel wanted to win and what he'd do to get the first spot. *We'll know tonight,* he thought.

Darrel left them, leaving the three extra passes with MacAttack to give to the other boys when they arrived.

"Pro practice session in ten minutes. You can get onto the field a bit later with those passes, but stay back from the track," he said, walking out of the press box. He added, "Remember, you're VIPs now."

"Can you believe we're *here?* I can't!" said Ricky.

"Can you believe we're going to *ride* that track tomorrow morning?" said Jeff.

"Can you believe how many double-burgers we'll have to eat to even *try* that double jump!" said MacAttack.

Their nervous laughter was silenced by the throaty roar of a 250cc motocross bike starting up far below them.

"Where is he?"

"Way over there in that tunnel!"

"It's a Honda!"

"It's Brent!"

This race was going to be Brent's race as he'd told all the boys at camp. Nothing and nobody, he'd said, would keep him from winning.

And now, as the first rider out onto the track for practice, he was going to do all he could to win. By gate time, he'd know the track better than anyone else.

Three sets of eyes followed closely from the press box as Brent made his first cautious lap of the newly built track. Four-hundred truckloads of dirt and three bulldozers had built it in twenty-four hours. Brent and his competitors had four hours to learn it before the gate dropped.

Standing on the pegs, Brent sized up the jumps, circling, and riding back to pick the best lift-off spots. He'd park his Honda and walk certain sections, then slowly continue. He pulled off and talked to his mechanic, who then ran out through the tunnel back to the pits. Other pro-class riders began arriving.

One rider, listed 53rd on the entry list, attacked the track from the word go, jumping high on his first practice lap. Going into a section of bumps, he found himself in trouble, not having picked a smooth line beforehand. His rear wheel shot sideways, he lost control and hit a haybale head on.

"Supercross tracks are deadly!" said Mac.

"That guy is obviously an also-ran," Jeff added.

By this time, Brent had started to pick up speed and was hitting the jumps at near racing-pace, checking for landing lines and turn-approaches.

"Watch how he goes sideways off that jump and lands already set-up for that tight turn!" said Ricky, wide-eyed.

"Yeah," said MacAttack, "but watch how he *doesn't* try the double-jump." And, sure enough, Brent simply rode over the two hills, not ready to jump them. Nor did any of the other riders.

"There's Darrel," Ricky pointed to the starting area.

Darrel joined in the practice, riding with caution and studying lines like he'd told his pupils to do a week earlier.

"It'll be excellent to see him and Brent fight it out tonight," said Ricky.

Later, when the first private practice session ended, the boys took the elevator back down to the press tunnel. MacAttack went to find the Baysville Crazies and Adam to give them their orange passes. Ricky and Jeff went out to the concourse.

They realized that it felt pretty good to walk through the gathering crowds with press passes on. They saw hundreds of kids their own age, lined up to buy tickets for seats on the top balcony, rear. They both realized that they were very fortunate.

"I bet we could get fifty bucks for these passes," whispered Jeff.

"I bet a hundred!" said Ricky, laughing.

The parking lot, which had been a vast asphalt prairie when they'd arrived, was quickly becoming a colorful sea of cars and people. Traffic attendants, with fluorescent vests, waved orange pointers like runway signallers. The turnstyle lines were jammed.

Ricky and Jeff walked past program vendors, T-shirt salesmen, and girls who gave away paper visors with a race sponsor's logo printed on them.

They arrived at the back of a crowd, mostly boys their own age, who pressed tightly against a chain-link fence.

"I'll bet these are the pro pits," said Jeff.

They were. Eager autograph seekers pushed programs, hats and bits of paper through the fence, calling on their favorite riders for signatures. Older fans watched intently as mechanics, in white coveralls, deftly fitted new tires and worked on suspension adjustments.

Ricky and Jeff watched too. They looked for Brent and saw him on the far side, sitting in the back of his box-van, talking with his mechanic and sipping apple juice.

"I wish we could go in there."

"Yeah. Me, too."

Then, in perfect unison, each boy looked at the other's orange pass and said, "We *can* go in there!"

They pushed eagerly past some unwilling fans, who seemed to resent the intrusion, and walked into the pits after a nod from the security guard.

Jeff felt his face go red with excitement and he smiled, thinking how the fans on the outside of the fence were all wishing they could do just what he was doing.

He and Ricky spent fifteen minutes walking through the pro pits. They were struck by the fact that the top riders, Brent's competitors, seemed to be the most at ease, even though they were under the most pressure to win.

Ricky walked to the back of Brent's van and said, "Winning isn't everything, it's the only thing!"

Brent smiled, not recognizing him, and continued his mechanical conference.

Ricky shrugged and backed off. "I guess he's got a lot on his mind."

A small loudspeaker crackled with an announcment, "Last pro practice before qualifier number one. . . ."

Jeff and Ricky found the tunnel that led to the field and walked down into it, through the dark recesses, past parked bulldozers and piles of crowd barriers. Photographers, covered with dangling lenses, ran to and fro. Officials with radio headsets held private conversations. Flagmen were being called to position.

Jeff couldn't believe the immensity of the stadium as seen from field-level. The white, air suspended roof seemed miles away, and the gathering crowd was too immense to comprehend. He'd been at a highschool football game once with six thousand fans, but that was nothing compared with this.

Trackside, he wished he had an extra set of eyes and a video camera or three. All around him the air was full of pro riders doing special, one-handed flights, cross-ups and table-top jumps, loosening up for the first race. A small knot of photographers waited by the double-jump. Practice time was show-off time.

Ricky looked at the double and said simply, "Never!"

The jump was much higher and longer than they'd imagined. Jeff even wondered if the pros would ever jump it.

Then, much to the delight of the crowd, who roared with approval, Jim Maxo, third in the standings, took a flight over the doubles.

"Easy as pie," said Jeff to no one in particular.

Now the pressure was on the other riders—jump it or lose. One after another tried it and only some of the slower riders backed off. Brent did it with a one-handed show-off maneuver. Darrel cleared the second hill with inches to spare, landing smoothly.

Jeff thought he'd heard someone call his name. He turned and looked into the crowd. Just then, he realized that he'd never been so public in all his life. If he tripped and fell, fifty thousand people would see it and laugh. He quickly became "Tension" Scott once more. Then, again he heard someone call his name.

He looked along the red railing in front of the first row. At the bottom of an aisle, leaning over the railing was Charlene, her brother Pete behind her.

"Jeff!" she called for the third time.

Jeff walked over, trying to act like being on the field was nothing, trying to lose the redness from his cheeks.

"Isn't this great?" exclaimed Charlene. "It must be wonderful to be down there. Who was it you said I should watch for?"

"Brent Wade. He's on a red bike, number 7. And Darrel Boyd, he was an instructor at camp. He's number 42, on a yellow bike. A Suzuki."

"And tomorrow, I'm the cheerleader for *you* guys," she said, waving an invisible pom pom. "By the way, where are the other guys?"

Jeff looked at Charlene, trying to decipher her question. "Mac's outside and Art's with his dad up in section 30, I think."

"And what about Adam?"

"I think he's feeling sick," said Jeff, feeling not so great himself.

As he said it, all went quiet. The crowd behind Charlene stood. The national anthem played, loud and echoing through the monstrous space.

The event had begun.

11
Surprise Finish!

As the last few bars of music died under a thunderous wave of cheering, Charlene and Jeff parted.

The air was charged with the sounds of racing. A blue haze rose from the tailpipes of the first set of qualifiers. Seeing it, the crowd cheered.

Jeff watched the man in white, the starter, who stood in turn one with a white "30 seconds" sign. He turned it sideways and twenty-five right wrists hit hard on the throttle. The gate dropped. The race was on!

The bikes roared into turn one, then simultaneously shut down for the corner, their roar echoing behind them.

This was Darrel's qualifier, but from Jeff's position at field level, it was difficult to see who had emerged from first-turn traffic in first place. As the riders worked their way around the serpentine track to his side, it became apparent that it *wasn't* Darrel.

Jim Maxo, the rider from San Francisco, had the lead—just barely—over the number one man in the standings, Bob McBride.

Jeff's sympathies went out to Darrel, who he could see back in the pack, about tenth. Being in the same qualifying race as Maxo and McBride cut his chances way down. He'd have to ride hard.

At least Brent's not in this race, Jeff thought. And he wondered what would happen if Brent and Darrel both qualified and had to race against each other in the final? Ricky and MacAttack had argued about it during the trip.

"Brent will eat him alive!" Ricky had said.

"Darrel might pull an upset. He's smarter." Mac had countered.

Jeff had sided with Ricky, but he still didn't know who was *really* the better rider, nor who he *wanted* to win.

However, before any of that could be decided, Darrel had to qualify by placing in the top five in his heat.

A near miss on the doubles slowed McBride to third, and a traffic jam in a rutted, sandy corner let Darrel slip by several racers to qualify with one lap left.

Jeff sighed with relief as Darrel rode by, headed for the pits. He gave Jeff the "thumbs up" as he coasted on, physically drained.

Darrel had been lucky. As a qualifier in heat one, he had time to rest before the all important final, the only race that mattered.

Brent, on the other hand, raced in the third qualifier and even though he ran away with it, winning unchallenged, he too was exhausted at the checkered flag and had less time to recover. Jeff wondered, *Maybe this evens the odds a little. Maybe Darrel does have a chance at beating him.*

During the intermission show, Jeff found MacAttack. He and the Baysville Crazies were busy posing on the starting line. Jim Thomas stood between Dave and Mac—upsidedown on his head.

Adam was shooting slides of them with his Nikon.

"This," announced MacAttack to Jeff and a few curious pro riders who looked on laughing, "is what Jim calls 'using his head'."

"Mind games!" said Jim, straining, with a red face.

The boys then took the elevator up to the press box. Darrel had suggested (correctly) that they would see the races better from "up top," and the Final was definitely *the* race to see.

The press box was crowded. Front row was jammed with people who were working. Newspaper reps talked to sports editors on private phones. Writers typed stories on computers sprung from plastic briefcases, and others scanned result sheets from a copy machine that whirred in the corner.

MacAttack scanned the big room, and said, "It looks like there are a lot of people who aren't press and shouldn't be in here taking up seats."

"Who?" said Adam, trying to recognize them.

"Us!"

They finally found some seats, in the second row, and they sent Jim Thomas to get the free pop that the sponsors had provided for the press.

Speculations about the outcome of this final filled the air.

The Baysville Crazies maintained that Bob McBride would take it. "After all," they said, "he's number one, the biggest winner this year!"

Ricky liked Jim Maxo and Brent Wade, both winners in their heats. "The scoreboard," he reminded them, "says that Brent turned the single fastest lap time tonight and Maxo was first to clear the Doubles."

MacAttack was undecided, but finally went with the under dog and chose Darrel. "After all," he argued, "he was only one second off Brent's pace and he was likely saving energy for the final. He's rested. And smart."

Jeff waited for Adam's opinion. Adam seemed to be a bundle of nerves and just shrugged his shoulders and sipped his pop. *He's probably nervous about the big confrontation with his dad tomorrow*, thought Jeff.

"I know for a fact who's going to win," said Jeff, "the guy who crosses the finish line first at the end of lap twenty, that's who!"

"My friends, the moment of truth!" said MacAttack, in his best "preacher" voice.

The whole stadium was standing now, like one person, all 60,000 pairs of eyes focused on the twenty-five riders lined up for the final event.

Riders conferred for the last time with their mechanics and trainers, looking at stop watches, talking about lines to turn on.

McBride, Maxo and the other five or so favorites sat quietly, professionally. They concentrated on the gate, rehearsing in their minds what they'd be doing in three minutes. Their trainers massaged their backs, keeping muscles loose.

For most of the riders this was, after all, pure business. Not only would the winner go away ten thousand dollars richer, but he would gain points leading to the series championship, collect more product endorsement contracts, and solidify his spot on the team he rode for.

Jeff silently wondered how many of the riders still felt that motocross was fun. Little by little he was beginning to feel for Adam.

The gate dropped. A thousand flashbulbs popped.

Bob McBride flew to the first turn like MacAttack to a Monster Burger. And to the delight of the six boys in the press box, Brent Wade nailed down second place.

Darrel was a victim of first turn traffic. An outside gate position had put him behind even before the race started. But he was persistent—with twelfth place out of turn one he was still in the running.

Bob and Brent set a blistery pace at the front of the pack, careening through the man-made obstacles, flying higher and farther off of the jumps than anyone had all evening. Bob was on the hot seat, feeling the pressure. Brent knew it, and was content to wait for a mistake, riding a bike length behind, watching his once-a-lap pit-board for warnings about challenges from behind.

This was what the crowd had paid for and driven miles for and waited in line for: two of the country's best racers putting on the show of the year, each riding on the ragged edge of control, a missed shift or misplaced wheel away from disaster.

By the midpoint of the race, Darrel was beginning to pick up positions, gaining advantage from his years of experience and training. One after another the young riders ahead of him fell prey to tricky jumps and tired legs.

A snarl-up at the corner before the double jump was all that he needed. Jim Maxo went down, taking fourth with him. Darrel rode along the streamers and went into third.

MacAttack and Jeff looked at each other, smiling in disbelief.

Ricky, shaking his head, said, "No way!"

Darrel was closing on Brent. Tired by his late qualifier and the frenzied front runner's pace, Brent was beginning to fade. He was beginning to lose his sharpness, and knowledgable eyes could detect it.

He was inches off on his landings now, dangerously close to losing it on the double jump.

Darrel knew it, and he knew that Maxo was gaining on him from the rear again.

Even the press-box crowd was on its feet now, cheering—some for Brent, some for Darrel, the new unknown factor.

Brent, out of desperation, dove low on a fast turn and cut inside Bob McBride. But his reactions were slow. He braked too late, ramming Bob from the side, taking them both into the trackside streamers, sending a wave of cheers and groans thundering around the stadium. In an instant, Darrel was by, into the lead!

MacAttack threw his cup into the air and let out a war cry, *"Kawumbah!"*

Brent and Bob, after the short delay, were after him again. The white, one-lap flag went out for Darrel. Fourteen turns and sixty-five seconds separated him from his first *big* win.

Jeff could see the scoreboards frantic search for a name to put beside the new leader's number. After all, Darrel Boyd had *never* led a supercross race in his life! He was an unknown quantity.

Brent had bested Bob McBride in the corner run-in. He was getting some scattered "boos" for what had appeared to be a dirty move, but he was in second place, hardly a bike length behind Darrel now.

They roared around the last turn, setting up for the long straight that led to the double-jump finish line.

Something strange happened.

Without apparent reason, Darrel backed off. He slowed to the point where jumping was out of the question.

In the meantime, Brent blasted by and cleared the jump, craning his neck at Darrel, ten feet below him. He landed cockeyed and wobbled for an instant. When he had regained his balance he threw his hands up in a gesture of stunned disbelief and coasted by the checkered flag.

The press box fell silent. MacAttack and his friends stared at Darrel who rode slowly off the track, "thumbs up" to the startled winner. The crowd was still on its feet, not knowing whether to cheer Brent or groan—a major upset in the making, then an intentional slow-down.

Quickly, then, the cluster of trackside reporters and photographers converged on the finish line for post-race interviews. Looking like a scene from a slapstick movie, they tripped over each other as half of them chased the winner and half went after Darrel. What had happened to number 42?

"I just can't believe it!" said Jim Thomas.

"He had it made in the shade!" said Mac.

"He is the ultimate no-mind!" added Ricky.

"He's pretty impressive," said Adam.

This comment turned a few heads and gathered some questioning looks. Adam had been pretty silent, but this comment made up for it.

"What do you mean 'impressive'? He had it in the bag and he backed off," Jeff said, in disbelief.

"Right, but it takes a real fine racer to do what he did," Adam began. "If he'd won, with Brent and Bob holding second and third, Brent wouldn't have gained enough points to have a chance at the season's title. Darrel wasn't even in the points race, so he let Brent by to give him a fighting chance at the end of the season. He knows—we all know—he could have won. He just proved that he practices what he preaches."

The boys were speechless. Realizing that Adam had hit the nail on the head, they felt a little guilty, but MacAttack broke the silence with a well-timed "Amen to that!"

After watching the awards ceremony (during which Darrel was applauded loudly for his sportsmanship) the boys talked to him briefly.

"But you *could* have won and nobody would be angry. You raced fair and square," said MacAttack.

"Look, Mac," said Darrel (as two magazine reporters held out mini-tape recorders to him), "winning this race means a lot more to Brent's career than it ever could to mine. I'm past my prime—he's a contender. Anyway, it's still the best placing and biggest pay check of my career. Like, I said, 'Winning is *not* the only thing!' Remember *that* saying from now on, okay?"

Then Darrel invited the boys to an early morning Mind Power session at the stadium before the amateur races the next day. They eagerly agreed.

Back at their motel, poolside, MacAttack led the

boys in some late-night antics. There was no further discussion about whether Darrel was as good a racer as Brent or not. There was no discussion because the answer had been clearly decided.

Adam and his dad, who were parked at the same motel with their motorhome, stopped in for a visit. Jeff's dad went out for coffee with Mr. Bylow.

"I hope they have a good talk," Mac whispered to Jeff. "Adam's still planning to fake sick tomorrow, but I'm praying he'll change his mind!"

Jeff remembered what his mother always told him—"Just pray about the problem and don't worry about it. . . ." *Good advice*, he thought, watching his friends ending the day with wild abandon. Their crazy pool war didn't give Jeff any time to worry about the big race the next day.

When Art arrived and heard their stories about life in the pressbox, he said, "You guys should be in bed. You've got to race in the morning!"

The Baysville Crazies replied by throwing him, fully clothed, into the pool.

Jeff laughed along with the rest. *This business of worrying is useless*, he was thinking. *Relaxing and enjoying life like this is a lot better*. He smiled at MacAttack and realized that his crazy friend had a good grasp on what the abundant Christian life was all about.

And, as he pondered this profound thought, his crazy friend rushed at him and forced him, kicking and wrestling, to join Art in the middle of the pool.

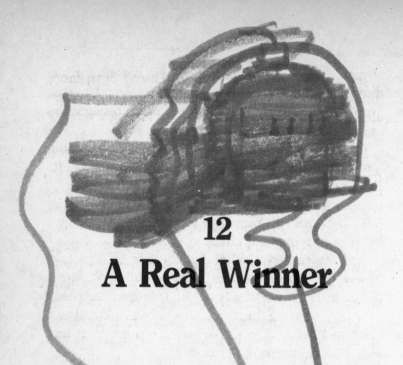

12
A Real Winner

"I don't ever separate the two things," said Darrel Boyd the next morning, sitting on the tailgate of his pickup at the stadium. "Life and racing are all part of the same ballgame. It's not much wonder that the Bible talks about our Christian life as a tough race. So how can I say one thing off the track and act another way during the race? It's not easy, though. It takes guts to always try to do what we know is right, and to think about the other guy first."

"Like what you did last night?" said Jeff, maybe a touch too eager to applaud his new hero.

"Well, that sort of thing, I guess."

Darrel stretched, looking at the reddish morning sky. He half-whispered, "It still would've been nice to keep the throttle on just twenty yards more!"

Jeff couldn't help but admire Darrel even more for admitting that. *He's an ordinary guy after-all—not a Super Christian. He just knows more about how to live life right*, he thought.

Darrel concluded the last Mind Power session with some racing advice. "Don't get blown away by the surroundings in there. It's just another race-track. You don't have to ride differently just because it's a stadium. Pretend you're at Three Hills."

"If we do that, then this guy will win by a long-shot," said MacAttack, slapping Adam on the back.

"Wait a minute," interrupted Ricky. "Why don't we have *Darrel* predict the winner of our race?"

A chorus of agreement put Darrel in a corner.

"The winner will be the rider who crosses the finish line first after ten laps!" said Darrel, mimicking Jeff's favorite line.

"Cop out!"

"Okay. All I can say is that I hope it's one of you guys. That's what all our training was for!"

The action in the stadium parking lot soon picked up as amateur riders from six states began to converge there. Trucks, vans and trailers of every description jockeyed for position where only the night before the professional pits had been.

After a mass practice session that resembled a New York traffic jam, the butterflies were building in all the rider's stomachs. Jeff, MacAttack and Jim Thomas took a walk back through the tunnel, join-ing dozens of rivals who were studying the course for fast lines. At the far side, a large group watched

117

the progress of a bulldozer operator as he shaved the sharp tips off the double jump hills.

"It's still deadly!" said Jeff.

"*Banzai* is the only answer!" replied MacAttack.

"No wonder they put this track in a football stadium," said Jim. "We'll have to make like NFL tackles to even survive one lap!"

MacAttack took the cue, picked up an empty pop can and made like a quarter back. Jeff hopped a string of Suzuki banners and ran downfield for the pass. "Throw me the long-bomb," he yelled, running backwards, hands positioned for the catch.

The can spun toward the stands. Grinning, Jeff jumped a haybale and leaped for the catch, like an outfielder at the wall. He missed it, and ended up draped sideways over the railing. The can landed in the fifth row and rattled down between the empty seats.

"Can we have a 'slo-mo' replay?" asked a familiar voice.

Jeff shook his head and straightened up. It was Ben Masters and a dozen or so kids from the youth group—and Charlene.

"Surprise!" they yelled in unison. Ben gave a quick explanation, "Charlene convinced us to come to the city for a special trip. She said *it just so happens* that Jeff and Mac and his friends are racing in the biggest event of their lives, so how could we resist? Jamestown cheering section at your command, sir!"

He noticed Charlene held back from the group.

When they'd moved off to talk to MacAttack, she leaned over the railing and held out the pop can he'd tried to catch earlier.

"I picked up on your fumble," she said. "Want me to ride your race for you as well?"

Coming from anyone else, it would almost have been an insult, but Charlene's smile turned it into an odd sort of compliment.

"When do the Jamestown killers race?" she asked.

"Killers? Chickens is more like it," said Jeff with his best sort of put-on humility. "We're fed to the lions in half an hour."

"Well, go for it you guys! Tell Adam and Ricky I'm cheering for them, too!"

Jeff didn't mind. He was pretty sure Adam wouldn't race anyway—in fact, he might be faking sick right now!

He looked at Charlene, saying nothing, just smiling. It was a comfortable smile, and it was reflected by the girl who was gradually becoming his friend. Jeff wondered which was more important to him now—winning a heart or winning a race. He realized that the choice was not so cut and dried.

In a voice that he hoped projected some drama, Jeff said quietly to Charlene, "I've got some racing to do." Then he turned and walked back to the pits, nearly tripping over the same haybale he'd just jumped like a wide receiver.

Revving engines and little clouds of exhaust told the story in the parking lot—it was race time. Goggles were being cleaned, shoulderpads adjusted, number plates polished.

Ricky and MacAttack were already suited up.

As Jeff approached, Ricky called out with enthusiasm, "The tide is turning our way!"

Jeff was puzzled.

"Superman Bylow is sick! He's pulled out of our race and gone into his mansion-on-wheels. Our big threat has choked out!"

Jeff glanced at MacAttack who nodded knowingly and said, "He's still got five minutes. Don't count your trophies before they shine, Rick."

MacAttack turned to Jeff, "Your dad went to talk to Adam and his dad. He thinks he can get Adam to race, but I don't know. Adam was determined to stay out and he's a good faker. He really *did* look sick!"

"Really?"

"Really. But let's get to the line."

"The Moment of Truth, right Mac?"

"Something like that."

Jeff tightened the strap on his helmet—one tug for Charlene, another for Adam. *For Adam? I must be losing it*, he thought, realizing that he really wished Adam would ride.

MacAttack had been right—Adam's absence would *kill* the race's importance.

Across the parking lot, down the ramp, through the tunnel, they pushed their bikes, Ricky, MacAttack, and Jeff, saying nothing, each consumed with his own thoughts.

Into the stadium, onto the field, up to the starting gate. Jeff was surprisingly relaxed and he felt confidence surging through him. No one else had jumped the deadly doubles, so he wouldn't have to worry about them. But, he wanted the starter to get the ball rolling, to drop the gate and kill the butterflies that were beginning to grow in his stomach.

MacAttack was not "The Jitters Killer" this time. He quietly eyed-up the gate, the riders beside him, and the line he would follow into turn one.

Ricky was swinging his arms, trying to relax the muscular knots in his shoulders.

Jeff scanned the crowd for Charlene and found her—standing with his dad. Both were smiling, cameras ready. *Whatever Dad said to Mr. Bylow, it's done now*, he thought.

The Baysville Crazies were on his right, talking to each other through plastic mouth-guards.

On his left was a rider on an Aprilla, a rare and expensive Italian race-bike, a rider Jeff had never seen before. "Gigliardi" was stitched on his shirt's back, "The Italian Battalion" on the back of his nylon racing pants.

The moment came at last and from this point on, Jeff realized, it was skill and determination—or nothing. He prayed a silent prayer—he left off worrying—his tension lessened—he watched the starter.

The two minute board went up and the starter circled his arm overhead, signaling for the gentlemen to start their engines. Screams of horsepower filled the air. Goggles snapped snugly into place, transmissions clicked into gear, the air filled with blue smoke and anticipation.

Adam wedged himself in beside Jeff and Jim Thomas. He looked at Jeff for an instant. Jeff, taken by surprise, responded in a surprising way. Without thinking, he gave Adam the "thumbs-up" and inched closer to Gigliardi, making space for his rival.

The board went sideways. The throttles reacted in a feverish escalation of pitch. And the gate dropped like a bomb.

The ride to the first turn was a swift and well-rehearsed one, and Jeff shifted by instinct. In the echoing, cavernous stadium, he couldn't hear his own engine.

He pulled out of turn-one traffic solidly in fifth spot, a length behind Dave Thomas, two spots behind MacAttack.

In a long, outdoor race, he'd be happy to sit contented in fifth and charge on the last lap, but in a supercross, he had to fight every turn, ride 101% every second.

Swinging wide of the goove in the sandy S-band, he passed Dave Thomas and aimed his sights on MacAttack. He caught a glimpse of the leaders, Gigliardi and Adam.

Rounding the band where mechanics and signallers stood, he saw Ricky, dejectedly looking at a stationery bike with no chain. He hadn't even completed one lap.

On, then, to the long straight, the finish-line

straight, the runway for the double-jump. Jeff knew he could pull ahead of Mac here, but would his buddy hang onto the throttle and attempt to jump the impossible obstacle?

Screaming his engine in sixth gear, Jeff pulled alongside MacAttack.

He's crazy enough to try it, Jeff thought as he inched ahead, into third spot. At the point of no return, he backed off.

MacAttack didn't. He had seen Gigliardi fly skyward and Adam had been forced to follow suit, so MacAttack pulled out the stops, yelling "Kawumbah" loud enough to be heard trackside.

It was, as Charlene related later, a pretty sight. MacAttack flew higher and farther than either Adam or the Italian Battalion, resembling a miniature, yellow space shuttle gone out of control. And it was, as Jeff's dad reported later, a pretty terrifying crash, as MacAttack overshot the landing ramp, and cartwheeled into a stack of haybales, unhurt but finished for the day. Art reported that Randy got up, bowed to the crowd and walked off the field like a true . . . maniac!

Jeff saw none of this but realized that MacAttack had been sidelined. He'd lost precious seconds by not jumping the doubles, but he was still in third place—and upright. He found that he could retain his position, regaining the seconds lost on the jump by riding the section of sandy bumps faster than the two leaders.

Lap after lap he did so, losing five bike-lengths at

123

the double jump, gaining them back on the sandy bumps. By the sixth lap, he realized he was gaining on Adam.

He wished he could see Charlene's reaction. *What's dad thinking?*

Lap seven, front straightway, Jeff pulled alongside Adam, heading for the double jump. Jim Thomas was in fourth now, hot on their rear fender, waiting for a mistake.

Jeff edged past Adam, screaming his Honda to the limit. If he'd had time to think about it, he would have realized that he'd come a long way from that day when Adam had made him look so *very* slow at Three Hills Raceway.

Jeff grabbed his brakes again. Adam kept sailing and shot skyward. Something about Adam's lift off was wrong. He might have been a little sideways, or maybe a bit out of position in his stance. Whatever it was, Jeff sensed disaster.

It came. Adam landed sideways on the downramp, skidded and washed out. Jim Thomas, seizing the opportunity, had also attempted a jump, but wobbled on his landing and rode off the track, tangled in banners.

Jeff rode through the gulley, unable to see over the landing ramp, and when he topped it, he ran straight into Adam's stalled bike, falling and tangling his handlebars in Adam's rear spokes.

Gigliardi disappeared into the sandy S-band. Charlene leaned over the rail, yelling encouragement to Jeff—or Adam—it was hard to tell which.

What Jeff did next he couldn't understand. He could hear the snarl of the next knot of riders approaching. He and Adam were about to lose their hard won positions. But instead of simply remounting and racing off, he found himself struggling to lift Adam's bike. He could see that Adam's leg was somehow caught under the bike so he couldn't get up without help. Once up, the leg fell free and Adam swung onto his bike yelling, "Thanks."

Jeff's own bike had stalled in the meantime and it was slow to start. He followed as quickly as he could but the whole time he found himself wondering what had just happened to him. That was a "Jeff" that even Jeff didn't know existed.

As he finally restarted his Honda, riders whizzed by on both sides, but Jeff realized he didn't even care about his own lost hopes of winning. At that point in time, he wanted nothing more than to see Adam regain his position and give Gigliardi a good race to the finish line.

He'd helped his rival, erasing his own chances in the same instant. But whatever had caused him to do it had now put him into a new race, one which he enjoyed with a fresh, total freedom. Jeff "Tension" Scott had crashed, but it wasn't "Tension" Scott who remounted.

From seventh place, Jeff could hardly tell what was happening at the front of the pack. He couldn't see the wheel-to-wheel battle between Gigliardi and Adam that had the crowd on its feet.

But he could see the white "last lap" flag as it

waved to him, and he could see the final straight-away as he pulled out onto it. Eighth place was far behind him—sixth was out of reach. Jeff, on his own, grinning behind his facemask, turned the throttle a notch higher than he had previously. He didn't touch his brakes and he flew spectacularly across the double-jump chasm.

To find that he could jump it without fear, to find that he could land smoothly as a pro, and to realize that he could have done so every lap and *maybe have won*, didn't bother Jeff. He only sensed a deeper, more complete joy because he had finally done it.

Adam, who had finished a wheel length behind Gigliardi, was waiting at the finish line. Even before Jeff could put his sidestand down, Adam had hold of his right arm, pushing it to the sky. "The Real Winner," he yelled, making more noise than anyone had ever heard Adam make before, and, Jeff laughing with some kind of moisture like tears in his eyes, said "Hey, the same to you."

Ricky was there too, after his early breakdown. His snapped chain was drooped around his neck like a garland of defeat. He held up the broken master-link and said, "How does that poem go, Jeff? Something about the thrill of victory and the agony of defeat?" He rolled his eyes and smiled a wide smile. "Nice guys always finish last, right Jeffrey?"

Then the rest of them arrived. Jeff's dad came over, and MacAttack, and Art, and Mr. Bylow. Gigliardi walked by with a real smile and a

126

"thumbs-up" salute. And Charlene handed Jeff his trophy—the pop can she'd caught earlier and kept.

As Jeff took it from her, watching her eyes all the time, she didn't let go, but said quietly, "Will you autograph it for me, Mr. Racer?"

"With pleasure," Jeff said, gripping the dented, hollow trophy, the strange symbol that stood for what *really* mattered to him now. "With pleasure!"